ALSO BY PHILIP R. CRAIG

Vineyard Enigma

First Light (with William G. Tapply)

Vineyard Shadows

Vineyard Blues

A Fatal Vineyard Season

A Shoot on Martha's Vineyard

A Deadly Vineyard Holiday

Death on a Vineyard Beach

A Case of Vineyard Poison

Off Season

Cliff Hanger

The Double Minded Men

The Woman Who Walked into the Sea

A Beautiful Place to Die

Gate of Ivory, Gate of Horn

A VINEYARD KILLING

A Martha's Vineyard Mystery

PHILIP R. CRAIG

SCRIBNER

New York London Toronto Sydney Singapore

Scribner
1230 Avenue of the Americas
New York, NY 10020

Copyright © 2003 by Philip R. Craig

SCRIBNER and design are trademarks
of Macmillan Library Reference USA, Inc., used under license
by Simon & Schuster, the publisher of this work.

For information regarding special discounts for bulk purchases,
please contact Simon & Schuster Special Sales at 1–800–456–6798
or business@simonandschuster.com

Text set in Baskerville

Manufactured in the United States of America

3 5 7 9 10 8 6 4

Library of Congress Cataloging-in-Publication Data
Craig, Philip R. 1933–
A Vineyard killing: a Martha's Vineyard mystery/Philip R. Craig.
p. cm.
1. Jackson, Jeff (Fictitious character)—Fiction. 2. Private investigators—
Massachusetts—Martha's Vineyard—Fiction. 3. Martha's Vineyard
(Mass.)—Fiction. I. Title.

PS3553.R23 V527 2003
813'.54—dc21
2002042878

ISBN 0-7432-0524-3

For my granddaughter,
Amelia Rae Craig,
whose eyes are as deep and blue as the sea.

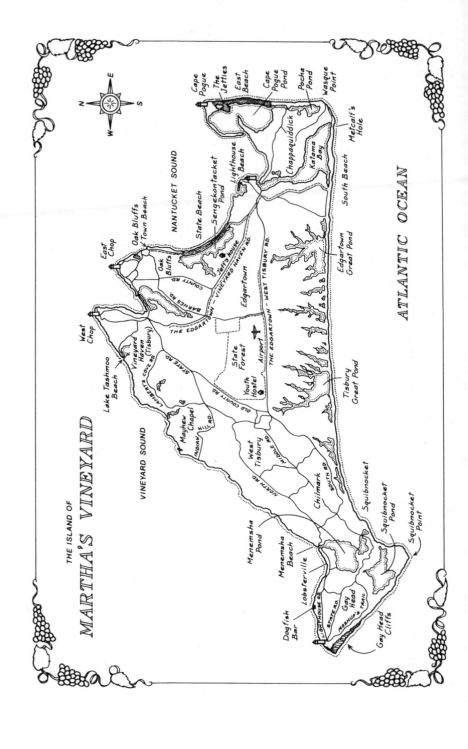

THE ISLAND OF
MARTHA'S VINEYARD

VINEYARD SOUND

NANTUCKET SOUND

ATLANTIC OCEAN

West Chop
East Chop
Oak Bluffs
Oak Bluffs Town Beach
Lake Tashmoo Beach
Vineyard Haven (Tisbury)
Lambert's Cove Rd
State Rd
Mayhew Chapel
Indian Hill Rd
Menemsha Pond
Menemsha Beach
Dogfish Bar
Lobsterville
Gay Head
Gay Head Cliffs
Lighthouse Rd
State Rd
Moshup's Trail
North Rd
Middle Rd
South Rd
West Tisbury
Chilmark
Squibnocket
Squibnocket Pond
Squibnocket Point
Old County Rd
State Forest
Youth Hostel
Airport
Tisbury Great Pond
Edgartown Great Pond
The Edgartown – West Tisbury Rd
Edgartown
Barnes Rd
County Rd
Vineyard Haven Rd
Jeff's House
State Beach
Sengekontacket Pond
Lighthouse Beach
Katama Bay
South Beach
Chappaquiddick
Cape Pogue Pond
Pocha Pond
Wasque Point
Metcalf's Hole
Cape Pogue
The Jetties
East Beach

N E S W

A VINEYARD KILLING

I hate and I love.
Why I do so, perhaps you ask.
I do not know, but I feel it and I am in torment.

—CATULLUS, *ODES*, LXXXV

— 1 —

Our children, Joshua and Diana, were over on the mainland for two days, being spoiled by Zee's mother and father, and Zee and I were having lunch in the E and E Deli with John and Mattie Skye. It was a sunny but chilly March day, with a cold wind blowing from the north.

Outside, the traffic at the dread five corners in Vineyard Haven was moving smoothly along. Such would not be the case when summer arrived and the street would be a slow-moving parking lot.

"Too bad the twins couldn't make it down with you," said Zee, wiping her lips.

"The girls have more interesting ways to spend their long weekend than being with their parents," said Mattie. "They're college women now."

I could remember when John and Mattie's daughters, Jen and Jill, were little girls, about the ages our children were now. I hadn't been able to tell them apart then, and I still couldn't. "They don't make a quesadilla as good as this one up in West-stock," I said.

"But Weststock has college men," explained Mattie. "Compared to that, even E and E food has insufficient appeal."

"You're brave to leave them alone up there for three days," said Zee.

I suspected that she was thinking of our Diana, who would be of interest to young men in another ten years or so. I shared her view, having begun worrying about just such boys shortly after Diana had been born.

"They're eighteen," said John, who made his living teaching medieval lit at Weststock College. "They're supposed to be grown-up enough to stay out of trouble."

I had never grown up that much, so said nothing about John's fantasy.

The front door opened and let in both some cold air and John Reilley, who looked carefully around the room, nodded slightly to me, and went to the counter to order.

I knew a folk song about a sailor named John Riley, but I didn't know much about this John Reilley. Two things I did know were that he always took a survey of a room before he entered it, and that he was a carpenter with the reputation of being good with his hands. It was an excellent reputation to have on an island that was awash with money being spent by people buying old houses, tearing them down, and then building massive new ones. John Reilley would never be out of work as long as he lived on Martha's Vineyard.

Almost immediately the door opened again and three other men came in, one limping slightly and carrying a silver-headed cane. After sweeping the room with their eyes, they followed John Reilley to the counter. Apparently today was a day when everybody was checking out delis before they came in. Strange.

"Well, well," said John Skye in a quiet voice. "I see

that even evil real estate developers are allowed in this joint."

My face apparently revealed my ignorance, because John added, "The one in the middle is Donald Fox, the boss of Saberfox. The one on his right is his little brother Paul. I don't know the guy with the cane."

"Ah," said Zee, straightening and frowning as she looked at Donald Fox. "The Savannah Swordsman himself, eh?"

I now glanced that way, too, for Fox's name was a headliner in the local press. The Fox brothers were tall, handsome men wearing expensive winter coats, but Donald's face was as hard as his brother's was gentle.

"The very same," said John. "Did I tell you that one of his minions has contacted us and made the now famous offer to purchase our place?"

"No, you didn't," said Zee, glancing at Mattie's angry face, "but Jeff and I have also been honored by a similar visit. The rep was a Mr. Albert Kirkland, complete with coat and tie and one of those little laptop computers that people carry around instead of briefcases these days. Jeff told him to take a hike."

"I was much nicer than that," I said. "I just told him we weren't interested in selling any land."

"And he said that it might be wise to reconsider since a lot of Vineyard land titles are pretty fuzzy and that Saberfox was doing extensive research in the Registry of Deeds."

"He left before any shots were fired," I said.

"What's scary," said Zee, "is that Saberfox has more money and lawyers than God and can out-spend almost anybody who has land he wants. Donald Fox has already ripped off half the people on the island and he's suing the other half."

"That's a slight exaggeration," I said. "He's mostly ripped off poor people, because the rich ones have as many lawyers as he does."

"Well, he's after Dodie Donawa's place for sure! He's done what he always does: he's offered her about a quarter of what the place is worth, and told her if she doesn't go along, he'll take her to court! She'll have to take his offer because she hasn't got the money to fight him. Disgusting! If Dave Donawa was still alive he'd probably shoot him!"

"Maybe somebody else will do it, dear."

"It wouldn't surprise me!"

"Down, Fang! I think we should change the subject before you get so mad you hurt yourself."

Zee glared at me, then at Fox, then back at me. She was not in a conciliatory mood. I turned to John. "What's your next project, now that you're finally done with *Gawain*?"

John Skye had been working for years on an ultimate authoritative translation of *Gawain and the Green Knight* and had at last finished it, whereupon he had immediately entered into a serious state of postpartum blues. This was a typical experience, he said, of writers who had just finished books. And there was only one way out of it: start a new one.

"Well, that Southern swashbuckler over there gives me one idea," he said. "Maybe I'll write a history of swordplay, from sharp sticks to modern fencing. Who better than me? After all, I dazzled them on the fencing strip when I was an undergraduate, and now that I'm almost a rich and famous literary scholar I'm the right man for the job."

"He's kidding about the rich and famous part, of course," said Mattie. "So far all he's gotten from *Gawain* is some good prepub commentary from other medievalists. He doesn't even have a publisher."

"But I'll get one," said John, waving a professorial hand. "Readers all over the world will be lined up to buy copies. I'll be on endless book tours. It's inevitable."

"I'm impressed by the way you can keep a straight face when you say that," said Zee. "I don't believe I know any rich and famous scholars."

"I'll be the first," said John. "Anyway, maybe I'll do the fencing book. Skeptics will claim that it won't make any money either, because there are only about two fencers left in the United States and neither of them can afford to buy a book. They'll say that it's a typical pointy-headed-intellectual project: a book no one will read, about a topic totally irrelevant to modern times. But what do they know?"

Fencing, it was true, was not a major sport in America. However, it did have its practitioners, including several who worked out twice a week in the high school gym as members of the Martha's Vineyard Fencing Club. I'd watched them a time or two myself, attracted, no doubt, by having seen a number of swashbuckling movies on late-night TV.

I'd even been persuaded to pick up a foil, but had rapidly realized that I had no more skill as a fencer than as a dancer, and that the cause for both failures was the same: feet that didn't move properly when called upon to do so. They worked well enough for other things, but not for dancing or fencing. The reason was elusive but the fact was certain.

John, on the other hand, had on his library wall a

battered mask centered on a triangled crossing of foil, épée, and saber that testified to his collegiate skill as a three-weapon man. Now, at sixty or so, he did his fencing with his forefinger, thrusting and parrying gracefully in thin air as he outlined his project.

"The first good part, of course, will be the research. I'll find out stuff I never knew. I'll go back into history as far as I can and trace sword fighting up to modern times, when training for combat turned into a sport."

"I presume you'll have a chapter on Errol Flynn and Douglas Fairbanks Junior," I said, "and another one on Zorro. They're the only fencers most people have ever heard of."

"A splendid idea. I'll have a chapter devoted to the movies, complete with lots of pictures. Flynn wasn't much of a fencer, by his own admission, but Cornell Wilde was a potential Olympian.

"Most people probably never heard of the real fencing champions—Nadi and Fonst and d'Oriola and the others—but they'll know about them when I win the Nobel Prize and fencing becomes the world's most popular sport. And they'll know about the guys who were around when I was slinging steel: Levis and Axelrod and Richards and Juan Diego Valentine."

"Are you going to mention our friend Donald Fox?" asked Mattie sourly. "Wasn't he America's only Olympic-gold-medalist fencer before he became a real estate tycoon?"

The tycoon under discussion, perhaps hearing his name, glanced her way with sharp, pitiless eyes. He stared at our table, then turned away.

Beyond him John Reilley looked at him thought-fully, then turned and walked out into the chilly street, carrying his order in a paper bag.

"Sure," said John Skye, "I'll mention Fox. I'll have to, because like him or not he was the most success-ful competitive fencer America has ever produced." He paused. "Some people who know fencing think he was the best saber man the world has produced in the last fifty years. Personally, though, I'd put my money on Juan Diego Valentine."

"Was he a world champion?" asked Zee.

"No," said John. "But I saw him in Spain when I was over there one summer. He was training for the Spanish Olympic team. He was the best I ever saw. Better than me, even, if you can imagine that."

"Inconceivable," said Mattie, rolling her eyes.

"What happened to him?" asked Zee.

John shrugged. "Who knows? I expected him to win the Olympic gold medal the next year, but he wasn't even on the Spanish team. Maybe he got hurt, or maybe he decided to enter a monastery. Things happen."

Across the room, Donald Fox and his companions took their paper bags of food and headed out the door.

John gestured. "Apparently Mr. Fox is so busy making money that he has to eat on the run just like ordinary human beings."

The rest of us turned to watch the men hunch their shoulders against the wind and walk across the street. They were about halfway across when I heard two little firecracker sounds off to the right and the man John had identified as Paul Fox stag-gered and fell. The man with the cane instantly muscled Donald Fox at a fast trot across the street to the shelter of a building on the corner.

I rose without thinking and headed for the door. "Call nine-one-one," I said to the boy behind the counter. "Tell them that a man's been shot."

"Wait!" cried Zee.

But I didn't wait. When I got to the street I glanced in the direction of the firecracker sounds, saw nothing, and ran out to the fallen man. I got my arms under him and dragged him back to shelter in front of the deli. He was white-faced and moaning between gritted teeth.

"Help is coming," I said. "Do you know where you're hit?"

He put a hand on the center of his chest. "Right here. It hurts. God damn!" He was gasping for breath.

I tore open his coat and saw two slugs half buried in a bulletproof vest.

"You're wearing armor."

"Yes."

"A fortunate choice of clothing. Lie still."

On the far side of the street the man with the cane had both arms around Donald Fox, holding him back.

"Stay right where you are till the cops get here," I called to them. "He's going to be okay." Then I looked at the deli door, where John Skye and Mattie were hanging on to Zee, and said, "You stay right there, too!" Mattie and John hung on harder.

I heard the first of the sirens. "You'll be fine," I said to Paul Fox, "but stay where you are until the medics get here."

His eyes were wide and full of fear.

— 2 —

The police station in Vineyard Haven faces the A&P parking lot, which was only a block away from the site of the shooting, but the cruisers were farther away, on patrol. Still, the police and medics were soon on the scene. Paul Fox was quickly taken to the hospital for further examination, while Donald Fox and the man with the cane were hurried out of sight, just in case the shootist wanted to take another crack at one of them.

The police were less concerned about my continued health, or that of Zee, John, and Mattie, who had by now joined me in the street. Dominic Agganis of the State Police, who had driven over from the barracks in Oak Bluffs, climbed from his cruiser, spoke for a while to a town cop, then came to where I stood. He didn't seem surprised to see me.

"Why is it that you and trouble are always in the same place at the same time?" he asked.

"We're not. The trouble was out here in the street and I was in the E and E having lunch."

"Okay, tell me what you know."

"I'll tell you what I know," said Zee. "I know my idiot husband ran out of a nice, safe deli into the street when there was a shooter on the loose! He could have gotten himself killed!"

"Whoever fired the shot was long gone by the time I got outside," I said soothingly.

"How do you know? I don't want to be a widow, and my children need a father! I don't ever want you to do anything like that again!"

"Mrs. Jackson, please," said Dom, holding up a big hand. "You can beat J.W. up later when you get home, but right now I need to talk with him."

"I don't want to beat him up, I just want him to be careful!"

My mouth opened and said, "I'm always careful, sweets."

"No, you're not!" I saw that her eyes were watery. I reached for her, but she brushed my hand aside. "Leave me alone! Give me your handkerchief! Come on, Mattie and John, we'll let Sergeant Agganis ask his questions." Wiping her angry eyes with my handkerchief, she led our friends back into the deli.

Dom watched her go. "You don't deserve her," he said, "and she certainly doesn't deserve the likes of you."

"True on both counts, probably."

"Okay, talk about what happened here. You can deal with your domestic problems later."

I told him what I'd heard, seen, and done. When I was through, he looked up the short street leading to the harbor. There were policemen moving around out by the beach. Some of them were on the porch of the Black Dog restaurant talking with people.

"You say you think the shot came from that way?"

"Yeah. Like I told the other cops, the sound seemed to come from that direction, although I could be wrong about that."

"You did take a chance, you know, coming outside like that."

"I never thought about it."

"You didn't see anybody when you went out?"

"Not a soul. I think there's a chance that the shootist might have been spotted by somebody at the Black Dog. They always have a good noon crowd."

"Trouble is that it's chilly and probably nobody was standing outside. Where do you figure the guy went?"

"I don't think he went along the beach past the Black Dog because there are windows on the harbor side and he would have been in plain view of whoever was there, so he probably went the other way. Not too many people back there in that direction."

"Or he could have just stepped inside the Black Dog and ordered himself some lunch."

"That, too."

"Any thoughts about the shooter?"

"Nothing original. Used a pistol at long range. Shot twice and hit the wrong guy then ran away. A pro would probably have gotten closer or used a long gun."

"You're sure he hit the wrong guy?"

"I'm not sure of anything, but most people would guess that Donald Fox was the target. A lot of people hate his guts. But maybe Paul Fox has been sleeping with somebody's wife when he was off duty."

Agganis grunted. "You sure the guy used a pistol?"

I shrugged. "It didn't sound like a rifle, and the slugs I saw looked to be about nine millimeter or so."

"The lab will check that out. So the shooter is mad enough to take a crack at Donald Fox with a pistol, but not so mad that he'll walk right up to him to do it, right?"

"Maybe. Not so mad he wants to get caught, I guess. How do you figure he knew where Fox would be?"

Agganis rubbed his big jaw. "Could be he followed Fox, saw him go into the E and E, and waited for him to come out."

"Could be, I guess. If so, he knows enough about the area to have an escape route."

"Yeah. Local boy or girl with a grudge and a gun?"

"Maybe."

"You sound skeptical."

"Shooter popped Paul, not Donald. Pretty bad shooting."

"Maybe he just wanted to kill a Fox. Any Fox."

"You mean like those people who gallop across the countryside in England yelling, 'Yoiks'? Could be, I guess, but you figure it out. You're the cop, not me. I gave all that up a long time ago."

"Look who's coming."

I turned and saw Donald Fox and the man with the cane walking toward us.

"I'm Donald Fox." Fox put out his hand.

I took it. "J. W. Jackson." We had a little squeezing match and called it a draw.

"Damned gutsy of you to come out to give Paul a hand. I appreciate it."

"The gunner was gone, and your brother probably got away with no more than bruises or maybe broken ribs."

"I never dreamed anybody would take a shot at me. Thank God Paul was wearing that vest. He's been after me to wear one, but up to now I thought it was nonsense."

"The car wasn't nonsense," said the man with the cane. "You have to be careful."

Fox put a hand on the man's shoulder. "You saved my life, Brad. I've not forgotten it and I won't. Gentlemen, this is Brad Hillborough, my colleague. Two years ago a woman tried to run me down with her car. Brad shoved me out of harm's way and took the hit himself. They don't come better than Brad."

Hillborough reddened slightly and shook hands. "I don't like this shooting," he said. "I can't save Donald from a bullet."

Fox turned to Agganis. "My brother is lucky to be alive. I want you to get the person who did this."

His last statement was voiced like an order, but Agganis didn't take orders from civilians, even a multimillionaire civilian with a reputation for tough business practices and for stepping on people who stood up to him.

"We plan to do that," said Dom without expression.

"Put every man you can spare on the job. I want that person caught!"

Agganis nodded and turned back to me. "What about John Reilley? You say he left the deli just before Mr. Fox's party went out. Did you see which way he went?"

"No."

"I'll have a talk with him." He turned to Fox. "You ever do any business on the island with a man named John Reilley?"

"Reilley? I wouldn't know. I have several agents working for me here and I don't know the names of all the people they've contacted. I'll check and get back to you." Fox looked at me. "Was Reilley the old man who was at the counter when we came in?"

"That was him."

"If he wasn't the gunman himself, maybe he saw someone." He put his hard eyes on Agganis. "Make sure you talk with Reilley."

Agganis never changed expression. "He's on my list. And speaking of lists, Mr. Fox, I'd like a list from you of all of the landowners your agents have contacted since they've been on the island. It's possible that one of them may know something useful."

"I'll talk with my people and give you whatever information seems relevant. I dislike making my business dealings public."

Agganis met Fox's flat stare with one of his own. "The more I know, the faster I can work. How many people knew you were going to be here for lunch? Who decided where you'd eat?"

Brad Hillborough frowned. "It was my idea. The food is good. The service is fast."

"Who else knew?"

Fox and Hillborough exchanged looks and shrugs.

"We'll try to find out and we'll let you know," said Fox. He turned back to me. "You risked your life for my brother. I thank you again for that."

"There was little risk."

"I'm going to the hospital now to check on his condition. You'll hear from me later." We shook hands once more, again running a quick strength test, then he turned and walked away.

"Lucky you," said Agganis. "You're going to hear from him again."

"And lucky you," I said. "You have someone to tell you how to do your job."

"It's hard for me to warm to Mr. Fox."

"They don't call him the Savannah Swordsman

for nothing. He was an Olympic champion and he's still a slasher and a gasher."

"I'd better go to work," said Dom, and walked away. I went to join Zee, John, and Mattie in the deli.

"Here," said Zee, handing me my handkerchief. "I'm sorry I yelled at you, but I meant it."

I pulled her against my chest. "I know. I'm sorry I worried you."

Her hair was sweet beneath my lips. "Let's go home and start a fire," I said. "It's chilly out. You guys, too. I'll mix us up some hot toddies and we can look at the whitecaps in the sound while we're warm and snug inside."

"An excellent idea," said John.

March is Zee's least favorite month, because it holds the promise of spring but rarely delivers. The worst of winter is past but the sea and its winds are still bone chilling, and the trees are still bare ruin'd choirs. You can walk the beaches, but you usually have to wear your woolies and down jacket when you do, and there are no bluefish or keeper bass to be caught. Zee was tired of being cold, and ready for warm weather that wouldn't quite come.

So sitting with friends before a warm fire was the proper thing for us to be doing that early afternoon, as we sipped toddies and digested our noon meal. We speculated about which of Fox's many enemies had shot his brother by mistake, if indeed it had been a mistake, and whether the assassination attempt would have any effect on Fox's island activities.

"The problem," said John, giving his drink an appreciative sip, "is the same one we'd have if some professor got killed in the faculty office building: too many suspects."

"Well, nobody's gotten killed yet," said Mattie. "And let's hope nobody will be."

"Some people deserve to be killed, dear," said John mildly. "Everybody knows that. The only argument is about who it should be. A lot of people would say that Mr. Donald Fox is a worthy candidate."

"At least one person apparently agrees with you," replied Mattie with a sigh.

The phone rang and Zee answered it. After a moment she said, "He's right here. Hold on." She gestured at me. "It's for you. It's Donald Fox."

— 3 —

I put the phone to my ear. "What can I do for you, Mr. Fox?"

"You can come up to the hospital so my brother can thank you in person."

"No need. I didn't do anything special."

"You took a big chance. He owes you for that, just as I do. We'd appreciate it if you'd come. Just for a few minutes."

I didn't want to go. "All right," I said. "I'll be up in about fifteen minutes, but it'll just be a quick visit."

"They're keeping him overnight as a precaution, but he'll be fine. We look forward to seeing you."

He rang off before I had a chance to say another word.

I looked at my buzzing phone and hung it up.

"Well?" said Zee.

"His brother wants to thank me in person," I said. "I couldn't figure out how to keep him from doing it. I'll be right back."

"Maybe Fox will reward you with a large check," said John.

"Or with one of the properties he steals from someone whose ancestors never triple-checked their land title," said Zee.

"Or both," I said. "Anyway, this won't take long."

"Just don't take the rum with you," said John.

I got into my winter coat and my Chinese rabbit-skin hat, climbed into my rusty old Land Cruiser, and drove to Oak Bluffs.

The Martha's Vineyard hospital constantly runs in red ink but somehow manages to stay open. Zee, who works there as an ER nurse, has seen about everything a nurse can see, from skinned knees to ODs to bullet wounds. Moped and bicycle accidents are especially popular catastrophes during the summer, but the other ER business occurs year-round. Paul Fox was one such piece of work.

I was directed to his room and found him in bed, with big brother Donald and Brad Hillborough standing alongside. Donald and I tested handshakes for the third time and once again called it a draw. I wondered if he used that powerful grip to establish dominance over whomever he met.

Brad Hillborough also shook hands. "Nice to see you again," he said. He showed his teeth in what I presumed was his version of a smile. He had keen blue eyes under slick black hair. He limped back a few steps, using his cane. Aside from his bad leg he had the look of an athlete, and I thought he had probably once been a graceful man.

I looked at Paul Fox. He seemed much younger than I'd taken him to be when I'd seen him earlier. He was pale and I thought he was still in shock or pain or under the influence of some medication. Or all three.

"I'm told you're going to be fine," I said. "I'm glad to hear it."

His smile was real. "Me, too. I'm glad they invented Kevlar. I want to thank you for helping me. You couldn't have known that the guy would be gone. You took a big chance. I'd like to pay you back somehow."

I shook my head. "I figured he'd have shot some more if he was still there. Anyway, I'm glad you're okay. You're in a dangerous line of work."

"Yeah, I guess so. I never had this happen to me before, though."

"Getting shot once is enough for a lifetime."

"You can say that again!" He laughed then grimaced as his bruised ribs protested.

"I hear that it's happened to you more than once, Mr. Jackson," said Donald Fox. I looked at him. "Everything is written down somewhere, if you know where to look," he explained. "I pay a lot of people to know where to seek information. They tell me that you were wounded in Vietnam, shot in Boston when you were on the police force there, then shot again several years ago by a young man here on the island."

It hadn't taken him long to dig up that dirt. If he knew that much, he probably also knew I now had no steady job but brought in money by fishing, caretaking houses, and doing a bit of this and that.

"I've gotten out of the target business," I said. "Now I live a quiet life."

"You can do me one more favor," said Paul Fox. "Persuade Don here to wear some Kevlar. Next time, the bullets might hit the man they were meant for." He put out a hand to his brother. "You know I'm talking sense, Don."

"I'm sending Paul back to company headquarters in Savannah," said Donald Fox. "I'd have done it before if I thought anyone would actually shoot at me. Most people are cowards, as you know. They rant and rave but they're all talk. Some of them push and shove or perhaps even swing a fist, and I don't need Paul to handle people like that. He's my only brother and I don't want him shot."

"Wait a minute," said Paul. "We've never talked about this."

"There's nothing to talk about. It's decided. When you get out of that bed you're going back to Savannah. You can work in the office there." Donald Fox turned from his brother to me. "Paul may be right about me needing some protection. I'm thinking of hiring a bodyguard. I've checked you out and you seem like the man for the job. The pay is excellent." He mentioned a figure that was excellent indeed.

"No thanks," I said.

"I want someone who knows the people on this island, someone who knows the crackpots. You were a policeman. You know the kind of people I mean, and you can handle a gun."

"I don't take money to shoot people."

"You killed that thief in Boston who shot you."

"I left the Boston PD and came down here to get away from all that."

"I owe you a debt. I'd like to pay it. It's a short-term job, if that makes any difference to you. I'm not asking you to go with me when I leave this island."

"Thanks, but no thanks."

He studied me. "Why not? The money's good. Better than you can make fishing and taking care of other people's houses."

So he knew about that, too. I said, "I won't work for you because I don't like your business."

He smiled coldly. "It's all legal."

"No big corporation's activities are all legal. The bigger it is, the more lawyers it needs. You have a lot of lawyers."

His face hardened. "I see that we can do no work together."

"If you want to reward me for doing nothing, you can go away and leave the Vineyard alone."

"I think I'll not do that. This is Treasure Island. In a few years the land I'm buying now will be worth ten times as much. I can afford to hold it until someone meets my price."

"All right, if you won't leave the island, you can call your dogs off Dodie Donawa. She's old and her house is all she has."

"I see that you're a sentimentalist. I don't know this Dodie Donawa, but if her title is not valid, it's no fault of mine."

"One of your people, a guy named Albert Kirkland, also came to see me. They're after my place, too."

"It's only business, Jackson. Nothing personal."

"It's bad business, and some of those crackpots you mentioned may think it's very personal."

"We'll see how tough they are in court. Or if they prefer an old-fashioned way of dealing with me, they can challenge me to a duel. Duels are quite illegal, of course, but arrangements could be made. I'll have choice of weapons, naturally, and the choice will be sabers."

He stepped back and assumed an on-guard position with an imaginary blade in his hand. Then, quick as a striking snake, the hand snapped forward toward my face and returned to the guard position. "Head cut," he said. "Touché. The conflict is resolved and honor is satisfied."

I had jerked away as the hand had come toward me, but I would have been far too slow if it had contained a weapon. I was both impressed and angry.

"There aren't many swords on Martha's Vineyard," I said, "but there are a lot of shotguns and some deer rifles. I think that the local duelists would use those weapons and that the encounter probably wouldn't take place at dawn beneath some giant elm." I glanced at his brother. "Paul, here, is lucky that whoever took that potshot wasn't a hunter. So are you."

"The would-be assassin was a coward," said Fox. "I have no fear of cowards."

"Cowards have killed many a man."

He looked at me with contempt. "You killed a woman. What does that make you?"

A thief I'd shot in Boston had indeed been a woman. I hadn't known that before she'd shot me and I'd shot back, but it would have made no difference if I had, since when people shoot at you their gender becomes irrelevant.

"It made me a fisherman instead of a cop," I said, "but it didn't make me into someone like you."

His eyes blazed but I turned away from them and looked down at his brother. "Go back to Savannah and get into some other line of work," I said. Then I nodded to Brad Hillborough and walked out of the room.

I drove home feeling a slight tremble in my hands as they held the steering wheel. By the time I got to the house the trembling had stopped.

Inside, the living room was bright and cozy in the dancing light of the fire, and Zee, Mattie, and John were relaxed and in good humor. Life as it should be rather than as it often is.

"You weren't gone long," said Zee. "What happened?"

"I was offered a job."

She frowned. "What kind of job?"

"The high-paying kind. I declined with thanks."

"Stop making a long story short and tell us everything," said John. "Sit down and I'll pour you a toddy. We've gotten ahead of you."

I sat in Archie Bunker's chair, accepted the drink, and related what had happened.

"You were right about it being a high-paying job," said Mattie, giving a whistle. "I didn't know bodyguards got such good salaries."

"I think Fox was trying to kill two birds with one stone: he needed a bodyguard and he wanted to do me a return favor for helping his brother. He's also the kind of guy who likes to be known as rich enough to overpay."

Mattie turned to her husband. "Say, maybe I should volunteer for the job. We can use money like that!"

"You've already got a job guarding my body, dear."

"But the salary is awful!"

"I'll double it tonight."

She fluttered her lashes. "It's a deal."

Zee looked at me. "Maybe I'll ask for a raise tonight."

"A pun, a pun! My purse, such as it is, will be open."

The next morning, Zee and I were having a last cup of coffee as we watched the cats, Oliver Underfoot and Velcro, have a pretend fight on the floor. It was apparently Velcro's turn to win because Oliver Underfoot suddenly scrambled to his paws and raced away into the living room. Velcro was deciding whether to chase him when the phone rang. It was Manny Fonseca, the island's most vehement gun fanatic and Zee's pistol-shooting instructor.

"Did you hear?"

"Hear what?"

"About Dodie Donawa!"

"What about Dodie Donawa?"

"She's in jail. They caught her up in the hospital with a pistol in her pocket looking for Donald Fox's brother."

— 4 —

Sure enough, Dodie was in the county jail in Edgartown. The Dukes County jail looks more like a big white house than a jail, but it's a jail just the same. When we went down there, we were with Norman Aylward, who was the closest thing we had to a family lawyer.

Dodie, fair, fat, and fifty, was hardly the type of person normally found in the gray-bar hotel.

"Dodie, we're going to get you out of here," said Zee.

"I've never been in jail before," cried Dodie. "I used to think that the people there probably deserved it, but now I know different. It was cold yesterday and I was wearing Dave's old winter coat. How was I supposed to know there was a pistol in one of the pockets?"

"You can tell us all about it after Norman gets you out of here," said Zee.

After Norman did that, the four of us went to our place for coffee.

"Are they going to put me back in there?" asked Dodie. "If they do I have to find somebody to take care of the cats."

"I'll try to keep you out," said Norman. "Now start from the beginning and tell us what happened."

Dodie bristled. "Well, it's because of that son of a

bitch Donald Fox! He's stealing my house! Says it isn't really mine! He's found some relative of some-body who owned the place a hundred years ago and he's paid them peanuts for what he says is their claim on the land and now he's going to take me to court unless I sell to him cheap! Says if I sell to him I can save myself a lot of trouble and get at least some money for the place instead of losing in court and getting nothing."

"Do you have a lawyer?" asked Norman.

"I can't afford a lawyer."

"You can't afford not to have one," said Zee. "Nor-man, how'd you like to be her lawyer? I've got some money and I'll be glad to pay your fee."

"Oh, I couldn't accept that," said Dodie.

"It's not just for you," said Zee. "Fox is after our place, too. Norman can work for both of us."

"We can talk about that after Mrs. Donawa tells us more about how she got arrested," said Norman.

I liked Norman. He was the only lawyer I knew on Martha's Vineyard who didn't wear a tie unless he was in court. He'd originally been recommended to us by our old friend Brady Coyne, who practices law in Boston to support his fly-fishing habit. Brady comes down to the island now and then to pursue the wily bluefish and bass with us as a change from angling for trout. If Brady worked on the island instead of up in America, I'd have called him to help Dodie, but Norman was a good second choice.

"Well, as you can guess," said Dodie, "I've been awfully upset by this business with Donald Fox. It just makes me sick. And then I find out that Maria has been going out with that other Fox! That Paul Fox! The nerve! His brother is trying to steal my house and Paul Fox is trying to steal my only daughter away from Rick Black. I just couldn't stand it! I threw on Dave's old coat and went right to the hospital to put a stop to that."

I thought that last choice of words was probably not one that she should repeat in court. "Wait a minute," I said. "How'd you know Paul Fox was in the hospital?"

"Because Maria works there, of course! She's a nurse. Didn't you know that?"

"I thought I'd told you," said Zee to me. "I guess I didn't."

"Well," said Dodie, "when they brought that Paul Fox in, that silly daughter of mine called me all teary and worried and it made me so mad, especially when she told me that he wasn't really shot very much, that I decided to go right over there and give both of those goddamned Foxes a piece of my mind! That Donald Fox was there, too, you know, so I could get to both of them at the same time!"

I had known Dodie for a long time, but I had never heard her use such language. I was impressed.

"And you took a pistol with you," I said.

"I didn't know I had it! Dave used to target-practice at the Rod and Gun Club, and he must have forgotten the gun when he hung up his coat. It wasn't a very big gun. A twenty-two, I think they said. I'm not like you, Zee; I don't know one gun from another. Anyway, that coat is heavy and has a lot of pockets and I was so mad I never even noticed the gun. That man Hillborough found it when he grabbed me."

"The jail keeper said it was unloaded," said Norman. "That's one good thing."

"Oh, I don't know," said Dodie. "If it had been

loaded and I'd known I had it, I could have shot all three of them. Good riddance!"

"Now, Dodie, you don't mean that," said Zee.

Dodie gave a great sigh. "No, I guess I don't."

"I'm sure you don't," said Norman. "Then what happened?"

"Then they called the police and Maria almost had hysterics and they took me to jail. And I was there until you got me out."

"Did you talk with the police?"

"They asked me what happened and I told them."

"Well," said Norman, "from now on don't say anything about this case to anyone. If anybody asks you anything, you tell them to talk with your lawyer."

"But I don't have a lawyer. I don't have any money to pay one."

"Lawyers do what's called pro bono work," said Norman. "That means they work for nothing. If you want, I'll be your attorney. If you don't want me, I can probably find another attorney for you. I recommend that you get one, in either case."

Dodie looked at Zee and me.

"He's already our lawyer," said Zee.

"All right," said Dodie. "You can be mine, too, Mr. Aylward. And to tell you the truth, I'm glad to have you help me. I never thought I'd spend a night in jail and I never want to spend another one there."

"I'll try to keep you out." He gave her his card. "You and I should go to my office now so I can get some more information and we can talk about our options."

"And then what will happen?"

"And then you'll go back home and take care of your cats and I'll get to work."

"What can you do?"

He stood. "First we'll see what we can do about this matter involving the pistol, then we'll have a look at the land title business."

"That awful man must have a thousand lawyers. What can you do?"

"I hesitate to use this metaphor with reference to lawyers," said Norman with a small smile, "but Samson slew a thousand Philistines with the jawbone of an ass. I may do as well with the book of law."

When they were gone, Zee looked at me. "I think Dodie is in good hands."

"Yes. Did you know Paul Fox was dating Maria Donawa?"

"No. Maria works in another part of the building, so I don't see much of her. She's a pretty girl and I imagine she dates a lot of men."

"Is she really as emotional as Dodie seemed to say?"

"It's hard not to be emotional when someone you love gets shot and your mother gets thrown in jail for threatening somebody with a gun. Besides, Dodie may be projecting her own emotion onto Maria."

True.

"At least," said Zee, "we can be pretty sure that Dodie didn't take that shot at Donald Fox. She was home when Maria phoned her about Paul." I said nothing, and after a few seconds Zee said, "Hmmmm. Maybe we don't know that. Dodie had plenty of time to drive home before the medics got Paul to the hospital."

"She's not one of the usual suspects," I said, "but you shouldn't take her off the long list."

"Some day someone else may take a shot at Donald Fox," said Zee. "He's made a lot of enemies here and he probably had a lot before he came. I don't think I'd like to have so many people hating me. I think I'd stop doing the rotten things he does."

"People who do rotten things don't think of them as rotten. I read somewhere that when Hitler was in his bunker and the end was near, he still thought that he was right to kill the Jews and that some day people would understand that and would thank him for it."

"That's sick."

"Maybe, but I don't think Donald Fox or his kind feel very guilty about what they do."

"What about Paul Fox? Is he the same way?"

"I don't know. He seems to be different."

"I know some people I don't like much, but none of them are evil like Donald Fox."

"I guess I don't think of Paul Fox as being evil."

It was a meaningless statement, since I rarely thought of anyone as being evil. Whenever I considered the nature of evil and good, I used the pine tree test: if a pine tree observed an act that men considered evil, would the pine tree consider it evil? I doubted that it would. I was pretty sure that no act had meaning except for the significance that human beings gave it. After my death, religious people seemed sure, I would discover I was wrong about that. But I wasn't dead yet.

Which was not the case with Albert Kirkland, as I learned the next day while reading the *Boston Globe*.

Kirkland had been found stabbed to death in the parking lot in back of the Fireside, one of Oak Bluffs' seediest but most popular bars. Kirkland was the Saberfox agent who had arrived at our door with an offer to buy our land for chicken feed and had left with a threat to get it for nothing.

People associated with Saberfox were taking some real hits lately. First Paul Fox and now Albert Kirkland. Another good reason to be glad I'd turned down Donald Fox's job offer.

A car came down our long, sandy driveway, and I went to the door to see who it might be. The car was a State Police cruiser and the driver was Dom Agganis.

He looked around, taking in the gardens and the view beyond them of Sengekontacket Pond, the far barrier beach, and the sound beyond.

"So this is your place. Not bad."

"We like it. Come and have some coffee. What brings you here?"

He followed me inside and sat down at the table. "Make the coffee black. I'm here on business. You know a guy named Albert Kirkland?"

"I know who he was. He worked for Saberfox. He was here a while back trying to buy this place cheap. We told him no sale. I was just reading that he got himself kacked last night."

"Yeah. Stabbed with a long-bladed knife. Looks like the stabber was sitting in the passenger seat. You got a long-bladed knife?"

I nodded toward the magnetic rack on the kitchen wall. "There's the long-bladed-knife collection. And we've got fish knives in the shed and tackle boxes."

"I'm talking with people who might have been mad at Kirkland," he said. "You're one of them. Where were you last night about eight?"

"I was right here."

"I suppose Zee and the kids were here with you."

"Actually, the kids were off-island, so they don't count as witnesses."

He drank more of his coffee. "You mentioned more knives out in the shed."

We went out to the shed behind the house and I showed him our several very sharp fish knives. Then we went back inside the house.

"What was Kirkland doing behind the Fireside?" I asked. "Besides getting himself killed, that is."

"Well you might ask. We're nosing around right now trying to find out if anybody saw him or the killer. It's a public place and the lot has pretty good light."

"But it was cold and there aren't too many people wandering the streets at night this time of year."

He nodded. "Yeah. People are inside, where it's warm. Whoever it is who's taking whacks at Fox's people has been lucky twice now. First up in Vineyard Haven and now in OB. Both times he did his work right in plain sight but nobody saw him. Kirkland was sitting in the driver's seat of his own Saberfox Range Rover when he bought it. He managed to get his door open and fall out onto the tarmac to die.

Almost like he didn't want to get too much blood on the company car."

"Thoughtful of him. Robbery, maybe? One of our local druggies might have needed money, and a guy driving a Range Rover would be a good target."

"His wallet was in his pocket, but we're nosing around the streets in case anybody knows something. So far they don't seem to."

"You talk like it might be the same guy who did Paul Fox."

"Who knows? However many people were involved, it would be quite a coincidence to have two unrelated killers out there whacking at Fox and his people."

"So because I'm mad at Fox for threatening to take my land I figured out a way to shoot Paul while I was having lunch and to stab Kirkland while I was home with Zee. Right?"

"Something like that. Don't get snippy. You know the routine. We're talking to a lot of people."

I did know the routine. When a crime is solved it's not done by a genius sitting in his house getting his clues from the newspapers and naming the villain by being smarter than the bumbling police; it's solved by hard work and, often, good luck. The cops start asking questions and keep at it and somewhere along the line learn something that takes them to the next thing until they finally think they have enough evidence to charge somebody.

"If I was going to the Fireside," I said, "it would be because I was thirsty or because I was meeting somebody."

"It's your kind of place, all right, but the Fireside isn't the sort of joint I'd expect one of Fox's people to habituate. I'd have thought they'd go to a classier watering hole. Kirkland was wearing a suit and tie when he bought it."

"Habituate," I said admiringly. "That's a word I never once heard used by my colleagues when I was a cop."

Agganis sighed. "I'm one of those new-breed policemen you may have heard about. The ones who can read and everything."

"Yeah. Well, I guess I wouldn't have thought that Kirkland was the Fireside type either. When he came to our place he was wearing a jacket and tie, too, and seemed like a bit of a prig. The only other people I've ever seen wearing ties around this island are lawyers. Maybe he was there to meet somebody more my type."

"Could be. We've talked with the bartender, but he didn't have much to contribute. He did say that he hadn't seen you for a while, so we know you weren't waiting for Kirkland inside."

"I'm a married man. I don't hang around bars as much as I used to do. You talk with Bonzo?"

"Bonzo was off duty last night. Home with his mother. You have any ideas about this that might help?"

"You check out Kirkland's quarters yet? Maybe something there might steer you in the right direction."

"We'll do that today. Donald Fox has made himself a lot of enemies since he got here, and he had a lot before he came. Probably the same can be said for the guys who work for him." Dom climbed to his feet. "Well, if you come up with any brainstorms, let me know."

"Meanwhile, am I on your short list of suspects?"

"No. Only the long list."

"Along with Zee and your mother. Anybody else?"

"Well, Dodie Donawa says Paul Fox stole Maria away from Rick Black, and Rick can be a bit of a hothead. So there's him. And of course there's Dodie herself."

"You're getting cynical in your declining years, Dom. See you later."

I followed him outside and watched him drive away.

Dom was a good cop and I had a lot of confidence in him. On the other hand, I didn't have total confidence in anybody, and I knew that many people had been found guilty of crimes they hadn't committed. It was possible, if not likely, that Dom might find reason to move me to his short list.

In every small community there are people who are, as the papers say, known to the police. The guy who gets shot at three in the morning is known to the police. The suspect is, too. The kid who beats up his girlfriend and steals from his mother may never be charged with anything because both the black-and-blue girl and Mom will swear he never did it, but he is known to the police because he's caught their attention before. The cops, especially small-town cops, almost always know the local perps and can usually guess who ransacked the empty house or drove the stolen car into a tree or smashed a series of mailboxes with a baseball bat as the batsman and his friends drove by in the night having a good time. They may not be able to prove it, but they know the people involved.

I had no desire to be known to the police in that

way, but it seemed possible that I could be. I was, after all, one of the few people who had been visited by Kirkland and had also been present at the shooting of Paul Fox. One event might have been coincidence and the other might have only been circumstance, but I didn't feel like waiting for a third that would indicate enemy action. I got into my winter coat and hat and drove to Oak Bluffs.

Oak Bluffs and Edgartown are the only two towns on the Vineyard where there are liquor stores and bars, so those are the towns where most of the fights happen. Edgartown likes to think of its bars as being classier than those in Oak Bluffs, and the other OB bars are certainly classier than the Fireside, which is at the low end of the drinking totem pole and has made little attempt to improve its image over the years.

In the barroom the smells of sweat, spilled beer, and tobacco smoke mixed with the faint scent of vomit and marijuana, and the toilets were rich with the odor of urine and disinfectants. I liked the place.

The back parking lot, where Kirkland had been killed, was off Kennebec Avenue, but that area would be cordoned off. However, since it was March there were parking places in front on Circuit Avenue, OB's honky-tonk main drag. I slid the old Land Cruiser into a slot.

The stores along the street, which would be bustling in June, were mostly closed up tight and the whole street had that look of emptiness that you find in all resort areas off-season. The Fireside, on the other hand, had a year-round clientele and never closed except when the Commonwealth of Massachusetts forced it to take a holiday. It was almost noon and somewhere the sun was over the yardarm. I went in.

Max, the bartender, was stacking beer in the cooler. I was his only customer. He straightened and wiped his hands on a towel.

"J.W. Haven't seen you for a while."

"I'm domesticated these days. Is Bonzo around?"

"He's bringing beer up from the cellar." Max leaned on the bar and lowered his voice. "You heard about what happened out back? Cops were here afterward asking questions. Wanted to know if you'd been here lately. I told them no."

"I heard about it. You know Kirkland?"

He shook his head. "They took me out to look at his face. Never saw a dead man before. Gave me the shakes. All that blood. I never knew there was so much blood in one man. No, I never saw the guy before, dead or alive. Not many suits and ties in here. I'd have remembered."

"You see anybody that night who looked like he was waiting for somebody?"

"Cops asked me that, too. I told them no. Just some of the regulars. I'd have thought that if Kirkland was meeting somebody, they'd meet inside, where it's warm. It was chilly last night."

"Who found the body?"

"Some woman driving down Kennebec spotted him on the ground. She thought he was passed out drunk and drove right to the police station complaining about me serving drunks. Damned old bitch. It wasn't whiskey that killed him, though."

"No."

He frowned. "Say, J.W., you think this is going to hurt business? Jesus, I hope not."

"I doubt it, Max. I think it might be the other way around."

"You think so? Jeez, I never thought of that. I guess you never know about people, do you?" He straightened and the frown went away. "You need anything from here, or did you just come to see Bonzo?"

"Draw me a Sam Adams."

He did that and I paid and took my glass down to the basement, where I found Bonzo about to bring up a case of Bud Light. Why anyone would choose to drink light beer I cannot understand, but like Max said, you never know about people.

"Bonzo," I said. "How are you doing?"

His mind was as dim as his smile was bright. "Say, J.W., I'm glad to see you! How's fishing?"

Long before I ever met him, Bonzo had, I'd been told, been a promising lad. But then he'd gotten hold of some bad acid that had turned him into a gentle child living in a grown man's body. He loved birdsongs and fishing and worked at the Fireside cleaning the floor and tables and muscling cases of beer and booze. His mother, a longtime teacher at the high school, loved him like the infant he would ever be.

"Fishing's not so good this time of year," I said, "but the bass and blues will be here in a couple of months and then you and I will go out and catch some of them."

"Say, that'll be great, J.W. I like fishing." His smile was curved like a fingernail moon.

"Bonzo, you must have heard about the man who was killed last night."

His smile was instantly gone and replaced by a

thoughtful frown. "Yeah, J.W. I heard about that. That's a bad thing, somebody getting killed like that. And right outside our door, too, right where I take the trash out to the barrels. My gosh, I wouldn't like to see that!"

"You weren't working last night, but do you think you ever saw the man around here before?"

He stared at me and thought as well as he could. "Well," he said at last, "like you say, I wasn't working here so I never seen him out there on the ground. But you know, I wonder if maybe I saw him another time. Max says he was wearing nice clothes. You know, a suit and a necktie and like that. That's different than what most people wear. And he wasn't one of the regular people who come here either. He was from off-island, Max says. And you know what?"

"What?"

"I seen a man like that out in the parking lot a day or two ago when I took trash out to the barrels. He was in a car talking with somebody."

I took a drink from my glass. "Who was he talking to?"

Bonzo shook his head. "I dunno, J.W. All I saw was the guy in the suit because I went by his side of the car. I never saw the other person."

— 6 —

"Was the man in the suit in the driver's seat or the passenger's seat?"

Bonzo thought hard. "He was the passenger. I wasn't really looking, you know what I mean? I mean I was just carrying trash out to the barrels and I just happened to notice a man in a suit as I went by and I remember him because of the suit. Nobody much wears suits, you know, unless you're going to a wedding. You got a suit, J.W.?"

"No, I don't. I rented a tux when I got married. What kind of car was it?"

"Gee, J.W., you want to know something? I got to tell you that I can't usually tell one kind of car from another these days, but this time was different. You know why? Because all those off-island people that just came here this winter drive the same kind of cars, and I saw one close up and it was one of those green Range Rovers that come from England." His face almost glowed. "And that's what the man was sitting in. A Range Rover. I don't know if it was green because the light wasn't too good, but it was a Range Rover, all right. When I was little I could tell the difference between lots of cars, but nowadays I usually don't know one kind from another, but that one was a Range Rover for sure!" He smiled and looked very happy. Good old Bonzo.

He wasn't the only one who couldn't tell one car from another these days. They almost all look alike to me, too.

"Had you ever seen the car before?"

"Well, like I said, I seen one of those Range Rovers close up once. It was parked right out there on Circuit Avenue so I looked it over. How much you think they cost, J.W.? A lot, I bet."

"More than I can afford, for sure. I don't suppose you remember the license plate of the one the man was sitting in."

"No, I sure don't. I bet it was from Georgia, though, because Max says all them people come from Georgia. If it was one of them special ones with letters that spell things, I bet I might have remembered because when I see them I like to try to figure out what they say, but I don't remember it at all so that means it was just ordinary." He beamed, delighted at his power of reasoning.

And that was all I could get from Bonzo. I finished my beer and thanked him and promised again to take him fishing when the blues came in, and left him to his work. At the bar Max now had a half dozen customers who had come in for lunch and a brew. I put my glass on the bar and left.

Of course the man Bonzo had seen might not have been Albert Kirkland at all, but I thought I should drop Bonzo's tale in Dom Agganis's ear just in case. I drove to the State Police office and found Officer Olive Otero sitting behind the desk.

Olive and I had a relationship characterized by mutual dislike that had started the instant we met and had continued ever since. When I tried to figure out why we felt that way, I was at a loss. It was one of those Dr. Fell things, and both of us seemed to work at making it worse.

Now she looked up at me and tapped her ballpoint pen on the form she'd been filling out. Her mouth was an unsmiling line that parted briefly as one word was spat out.

"Well?"

I looked at the form. "If you need any help with the big words, I'll be glad to help."

"I don't need any help of any kind from you. What do you want?"

"Actually, I want to talk with your boss. Remember him? The guy who tells you what to do?"

"He's not here. He's out asking questions about a guy named Kirkland who got himself killed. In fact, I think you were on his list of people who might know something. No surprise there. You're always in the middle of things that smell bad."

"Try to restrain yourself, Olive. You might burst a blood vessel. I have a message for Dom, and I'm going to leave it with you. You'll want to write this down because it's more than one sentence. Are you ready?"

"I doubt if Sergeant Agganis needs to hear anything you have to say."

"I don't expect you to understand anything more complicated than tying your shoes, Olive, but I think Dom might. Ready or not, here I come."

She opened a drawer and brought out a mini tape recorder. "I'd better use this. Your gibberish will need translation, and I'm sure as hell not up to it." She punched a button and sat back. "Shoot."

I told the machine what I'd learned from Bonzo. When I was through, Olive said, "Is that all?"

"That's all."

She shut off the machine. "It's not much," she said, but she was thinking.

"If Dom can come up with a photo of Kirkland, he can show it to Bonzo, maybe Bonzo can ID him as the guy in the car."

"We don't need you telling us how to do our jobs. If you don't have anything else to say, the door is right over there. And stay out of police business!"

"Say thank you, Olive."

"Thank you and good-bye, emphasis on *good-bye*."

I glanced back as I went out. Olive was rewinding the tape, looking thoughtful.

In spite of our mutual hostility, I knew she had to be good at her work or else Dom would have long since figured out a way to get rid of her. By the time she finished replaying the tape I was pretty sure that she'd be considering the same possibilities that I was: that if the guy Bonzo had seen had been Kirkland, Kirkland had been in the parking lot twice and both times on purpose rather than by chance.

Like me, she might also go further and guess that the parking lot had been chosen because somebody knew it would be a pretty quiet spot this time of year and because Kirkland, an off-islander, knew he'd probably not be recognized even if somebody did see him there.

The questions I couldn't guess at were why the two people were meeting and whether the driver the first time was later the killer. Could be, since Kirkland may have been a passenger the first time and was definitely the driver when he was killed. Still, it was a start. There weren't that many green Range Rovers on the island, and most of them belonged to

Saberfox. Of course, even if the man Bonzo had seen had indeed been Kirkland, it didn't necessarily mean anything.

But it felt like it did.

I drove home and planted peas. On Martha's Vineyard you plant your peas in March, so when other early-spring gardeners meet you and say, "Gotcher peas in yet?" you can say, "Yes." By June, just after you've finished eating the last of your asparagus, you can start eating fresh peas and pea pods. And not much later you can be eating your beans. Gardens are terrific. God was being pretty vindictive when he threw Adam and Eve out of theirs. No wonder there are so many people mad at Her.

I met Joshua and Diana when they came off the ferry not long before Zee came home from work, and all of us had some hot cocoa and cookies to keep us from starving before supper.

"Pa?"

"What, Josh?"

"When's school going to be out?"

"In June. That's about three more months. Why?"

"I'm tired of studying. I want to go to the beach."

"Me, too, Pa." Diana the huntress, ever on the prowl for more food, reached for another cookie.

"You'll freeze your bippies if you go to the beach these days. It's cold out there."

"No, it's not."

"If you don't think so, put on your bathing suits and go out and sit in the yard for a while."

The children looked at each other with happy, surprised expressions.

"Uh-oh," said Zee. "Now you've done it. It's too cold, kids. You'll get sick."

"Being cold doesn't make you sick," I said. "You can freeze to death, but that's not being sick."

"Can we really do it?" asked Joshua.

"Pa said we could, so we can!" replied his little sister, swallowing the last of her cookie and climbing off her chair.

A stormy cloud formed above Zee's head.

"You have to wear just your bathing suits," I said, "and you have to do it right now while there's enough sunlight for us to find your bodies if you die of cold before you can get back inside on your own."

"Come on!" The kids ran to their rooms.

"I don't approve of this," said frowning Zee.

"They won't be out long. It's chilly out there."

"If they get sick I'll never let you hear the end of it!"

"Come on into the living room with me. We can snuggle in front of the fire while our children freeze to death outside."

"It's not funny, Magee."

"Come on." I reached for her hand.

We were in front of the living room stove when our offspring, wearing their bathing suits, came running from their rooms.

"Now, you come in when we call you," said their mother firmly.

"Okay, Ma. Come on, Diana!"

They went out.

"I don't like this," said Zee.

They were back in five minutes, shivering and going immediately to warm themselves at the stove.

"It's freezing out there, Pa! We were like ice cubes!"

"It's cool, all right. Now go get into your robes and slippers."

"Pa?"

"What, Diana?"

"Can I have another cookie?"

"Just one."

They went off.

"You're a trial," said Zee, putting her dark head against my shoulder.

I moved my arm and put it around her, cupping a breast with my hand. "You're not so bad yourself."

She put her hand over mine. "Guess who's courting Dodie Donawa."

"George W. Bush?"

"No! John Reilley. I got it today from Dodie herself. She says John seems to be serious, too. I think it's wonderful. John is a good guy and a good worker and Dodie needs a man in her life."

"All red-blooded women need manly men in their lives. You're a classic example."

She got closer. "Yes, I am. And men need women. You're a classic example."

"Two classics in the same house."

"And maybe there'll be one more in Dodie's house before long."

"Why not in John's house?"

"I'm not sure that John has a house. If he does, I don't know where it is."

"Well, he lives somewhere."

"Do you know where?"

"No. Anyway, they can live in Dodie's house if they want to. So you think John is a good guy, eh?"

"Sure. What's more important is that Dodie thinks so, too."

I considered that confidence for a while, then reviewed everything I personally knew about John Reilley. It didn't amount to much: he surveyed rooms before he entered them, he was soft-spoken on the rare occasions that he had something to say, he had the reputation of being a fine, dependable carpenter, and he rode a moped wherever he went, winter and summer. I doubted if Zee knew much more.

If ignorance was bliss, Zee and I were a happy pair.

The snow fell first in great soft flakes, then switched to sleet and then to rain driven hard by a cold east wind. The leak in the corner of the living room that always dripped when there was a wet northeaster and never at any other time was plinking into the bucket I had on the floor. That leak had outfoxed me for months. I'd climbed on the roof with tar several times and had plugged every place I could imagine the water coming through, but the very next time a strong sea wind blew in rain, the leak leaked again. Blast and drat!

The kids had gone off to school bundled in wool and waterproof jackets, Zee was at work, and I was alone with the pesky, plinking leak and a final cup of breakfast coffee, thinking about the coming need to split more wood for the heating stove in the living room. When you lived as I did, you used your wood for fuel just as you used your garden and the sea for food. It takes work to live the simple life.

When the phone rang the snow had been washed from the cold ground but the rain continued to whip through the barren trees and slap against the windowpanes. March weather. I picked up the receiver. It was a voice I did not know.

"Hi, is this Mr. Jackson?"

A telephone sales pitch so early in the morning?

Some poor soul trying to sell me a condo? What a sorry way to try to make a living.

"Yes," I said.

"This is Maria Donawa. My mom says you helped get her out of jail. I wanted to thank you."

"I didn't have much to do with it, but I'm glad she's out. Dodie never struck me as the hoosegow type."

"I agree. From now on she'll be sure to check the pockets of the coat she's wearing before she goes to yell at somebody."

"A good policy."

"I need to talk to someone who's a friend of hers. I heard that you used to be a policeman, and that puts you at the top of the list. Can I come by for a few minutes and talk with you? Mom's here, in the next room, and I'd like to talk with you in private. I need some advice."

Women's best friends and confidantes are usually other women, so I was a little surprised.

"What about?"

"Can I tell you when I see you?"

"Do you know how to get here?"

"Your mailbox is at the head of your driveway, isn't it? On the left, just beyond Felix Neck, coming from Vineyard Haven?"

"That's it."

"Thanks a lot. I'll be right down."

As I hung up, I considered what I knew about Maria Donawa. She was a nurse, a slim young woman of middle height, with her mother's yellow hair and independent spirit. Aside from that, I knew she'd started dating Paul Fox, thereby infuriating her mother. That was about it.

I couldn't imagine what she wanted to talk about. A half hour later, I found out.

"It's John Reilley," said Maria, accepting a cup of tea as we sat in front of the living room fire. The rain lashed against the windows and drummed on the roof. In the far corner of the room, drops of water splanked steadily into the bucket.

"What about him?"

"He's courting Mom. He spends more and more time with her. I think they're getting serious. It worries me."

"Your mother is a smart, grown-up woman."

She shook her head. "You don't know how silly grown-up women can be sometimes. She doesn't know a thing about him. He comes to see her and she just beams and I swear her brain gets turned right off! Maybe he's dangerous or one of those men who lives off women. I think he's about to move in with us. I want to know more about him. Is he a gigolo or is he serious?"

"You're worried about your mother and John Reilley, and she's worried about you and Paul Fox."

She shook her head. "She's mad at Paul because of Donald. She liked Paul just fine until she learned his last name. When he came to the house the first time, she was happy because she thinks I should be settling down and I didn't seem to be doing that with Rick."

"That would be Rick Black, I presume."

"Yes. Rick is the guy I've been going with lately. You know him? He just got himself a new pickup a couple of days ago, but until then he used to drive a beat-up old Land Cruiser like yours. You must have seen it."

"I remember seeing it."

"He's a carpenter. We went to high school together and we've been dating. Mom likes him. She feeds him good meals when he comes by and she even loaned him her car when he still owned the old Toyota and it went on the blink. But Rick isn't ready to settle down, so when Paul asked me out I said yes. When he showed up at our door the first time, Mom was just as nice as pie. Then later, when she found out his last name, she blew her stack and you know what happened after that."

"Pistol-packing Momma got sent to the county pen."

She nodded. "Exactly. Gives you some idea about how her feelings can get between her and her brain. The same thing happens when John Reilley shows up. She gets all mellow and fluttery and stops thinking."

"What advice do you want from me? I don't write a column for the lovelorn."

She looked at me. "I know. I guess I don't really want advice. What I want is somebody to find out what kind of guy John Reilley is. If he's as nice as he seems, that'll be fine. But if he isn't I want to know about it right now, before he and Mom get too close." She hesitated, then said, "I'd like to hire you to investigate him."

I sipped my tea while I thought about that idea.

"I can give you the name of a good private investigation agency," I said. "They'll do the job better than I can."

"I don't need his life story. I just want to know enough to be sure that my mother isn't hooking up with some questionable character."

"A private investigator is your best bet."

"I want somebody who has Mom's interests at heart. I don't want to hire some stranger. I don't even know where John Reilley lives, for crying out loud."

"Zee and I just mentioned that the other day."

"You, too? Don't you think it's funny that none of us know where he lives?"

"I don't know where most people live, but it's generally not too hard to find out. The easiest way is just to ask him or look in the phone book."

"He doesn't have a phone, but Mom says he told her he lives just over the West Tisbury line, off North Road."

"Don't you believe him?"

"I drove up there and couldn't find a mailbox with his name on it."

"A lot of people don't have mailboxes. He probably gets his mail at the PO."

"Then I went up to the town hall in West Tisbury. They don't have any records about him. He's not on the tax rolls or the voting rolls or anywhere else." She frowned over her cup of tea.

"It sounds like you're already doing what you want me to do."

"I have to work and, besides, you can do it better. You were a policeman."

"I wore a uniform. I wasn't a detective. If you want to know what sort of guy he is, you should talk with the people he works with and with his friends."

"I don't know his friends or where he works."

Just to be sure, I got up and got the phone book. There was no John Reilley listed in the book. I called directory information and learned that the operator knew of no listing for a John Reilley.

A minor mystery. I felt my curiosity rise as I listened to the rain. Maria's face showed genuine worry.

"I can pay you a little," she said.

"No, you can't," I said, making my decision. "All right, I'll see what I can dig up. I know John well enough to talk to him. I'll let you know what I find out."

She looked only barely less worried than before, but put a smile on her face. "Thank you. I just want to be sure that Mom isn't going to get hurt."

There is no avoiding hurt. To live is to suffer, as the Buddha observed.

"We'll try to keep that from happening," I said.

She got into her wet raincoat and went out into the storm, running to her car as the wind tugged at her umbrella.

When she was gone I thought about John Reilley. I'd once worked briefly with him on a job. He was about sixty years old and had been on the island for a while, supporting himself by working as a carpenter either alone or on various construction crews. He always rode a moped with his toolbox lashed behind the seat.

He was a lean man of medium height who worked with great economy of energy, never seeming to exert himself or hurry, yet always getting the job done in that graceful, aesthetic way of all people who are good at their jobs. He had sharp eyes and walked easily and smoothly in spite of his accumulating years.

He favored camouflage clothing, wearing green tints in the summer and brown and white in the winter. Why, I could not guess, but sartorial sensitivity is not one of my strengths, as my thrift shop duds clearly indicate.

If he had friends, I didn't know who they were, but I didn't think it would be hard to find them or anything else about John that Maria might want to know. John had been on the island for some time, after all, and nobody lives anywhere that long without becoming known to at least some people. It was just a matter of finding them.

But it was too wet and cold to go out hunting them right then. Instead, I went back to the phone book. I realized as I did that I enjoyed nosing around in other people's business, and the realization made me a little uneasy. But not uneasy enough to stop snooping. I opened the book.

— 8 —

I talked with people in the town halls of all of the Vineyard's six villages. It took quite a while, and when I was through I knew that John Reilley paid no local taxes on the island and was not registered to vote.

I tried the registry of motor vehicles. John didn't own a car. No surprise there; you don't need a license to drive a moped.

I tried the post offices in the various towns and finally learned something. John had a box in the Vineyard Haven PO. That was helpful because in order to get a PO box you have to have an address that the post office people can verify. The problem was that the PO won't give you the address of one of its customers unless you have a legit reason to get it, such as a warrant or a summons. I had neither, of course, but I had something even better: a PO employee for whom I'd once done an invaluable favor. I had taken her fishing and she'd nailed a thirty-pound bass. She owed me a lot, and paid me with the address.

I didn't have high expectations of benefiting from this information because, according to my source, John had gotten his box years before. But sometimes things work out, so I got into a heavy sweater and my foul-weather gear and drove to Vineyard Haven. I needed the sweater because the heater in my old Land Cruiser doesn't work too well.

The address John had given the PO was an upstairs apartment just off State Road in one of the village's less attractive neighborhoods. I climbed the outside staircase, ducking against the rain, and knocked at the door.

After a while, a woman peeked at me through the window and decided I was trusty-looking enough to risk opening the door. She looked tired, and behind her I could hear a baby crying. I told her I was looking for John Reilley. She said she had never heard of him. I asked her how long she'd lived there and she said since last fall. I asked her if it was a winter rental and she said yes and that she and her family had to get out by June. When she said that, her voice was sad and angry but resigned.

It was a familiar situation on the island. You can get a winter rental fairly cheaply, but you have to leave in late spring so the landlord can rent the place for a fortune during the summer, when people will pay anything to stay on Martha's Vineyard. This place looked like the kind that college kids would rent while they worked and played between semesters. Three or four of them would officially rent the apartment, then another dozen would move in and share the expenses. They would all find jobs and promise to stay at them until Labor Day, but in mid-August they would quit so they could spend the last two weeks of the summer enjoying sun, surf, sand, and sex before heading back to school.

I asked her for the landlord's name and address.

She gave me a curious look. "You going to rent this dump?"

"No. I'm just trying to find John Reilley."

"He in some kind of trouble? You some kind of cop?"

"He isn't in any trouble that I know of. He used to live here, and I'd like to find him. It's just a personal matter."

She gave me the landlord's name and address and I walked back down the stairs through the rain.

The landlord was a realtor who had an office on Main Street. Since it was March I actually found a parking space not far away.

In the office I learned that John Reilley hadn't lived in the apartment for years. He'd rented it for one winter then moved out in June. The people in the office had no idea where he lived now.

I walked up to the Vineyard Haven National Bank and went into Hazel Fine's office. Hazel was wearing bankers' clothes adorned with a simple lapel pin in the shape of a scallop shell. Her dark hair looked newly cut and shaped. She rose, smiling, when I peeked in her door.

"J.W.! Come in. How's the family?"

"Everybody's fine. Both kids are in school, Zee's at the hospital, and I'm the only one with time to wander around and interrupt bankers at work. I can see that you're doing well. How's Mary?"

Hazel and Mary Coffin had lived together for years in a house within walking distance of the bank. They were a happy, creative pair who had played Baroque music at Zee's and my wedding. Hazel was my contact with the world of banking and finance, about which I knew next to nothing and would never know more, being afflicted with the equivalency of color blindness with regard to money. I just didn't get it.

Hazel waved me to a chair. "Mary's just fine and you always were good at avoiding steady work. So Joshua and Diana are both in school. Boy, time does fly, doesn't it? What brings you out in this weather? You need a loan?"

"No, I'm too cheap to need a loan. I never buy anything that costs enough for me to have to borrow money. What I want is an opinion and some information."

"I'm strong on opinion. Let's start there."

"What do you think of this business with Donald Fox? Is he actually going to be able to get his hands on island properties by doing what he's doing?"

She put her slender fingers together. "Did he make an offer on your place?"

"His agent did. Albert Kirkland, the guy who got himself killed behind the Fireside a couple of days back."

She frowned. "Does that put you on the suspect list?"

I shrugged. "I think everybody's on the list right now."

"Did Kirkland make the usual pitch? An offer to buy your place for a quarter of what it's worth and a threat to take it for even less if you don't sell?"

"That's the normal Saberfox MO, as I understand it. Is it a legit business practice?"

She allowed herself a thin smile. "Legit business practices are any practices that work, as far as the businessmen who practice them are concerned.

Sometimes the courts take a different view, but as far as I know Donald Fox is doing just fine. He's got more high-powered lawyers than the federal government and they've fended off everybody who's had the nerve to think about suing Fox."

"My impression is that he always bluffs first."

"I think that's right. He stays away from people with as much money and as many lawyers as he has, but he comes on strong and tries to scare normal people into selling. When that works, it saves him both money and time. But if it doesn't work, he puts his people to work on old land-sale records. Sometimes they find enough mistakes to get their hands on property, and in a place like this island, where land is worth more than gold, he's going to make some money. He's smart."

"And legal."

She shrugged. "So far nobody's been able to prove that he isn't. I hope for your sake that your deeds are good."

Me, too. Maybe I should get in touch with Brady Coyne, up in Boston, I mused. Paperwork for rich clients was his specialty. I wasn't rich, but I could probably tempt him to check out my deeds by offering him a fishing weekend in late May, when the bluefish would be in. Brady had an incurable addiction to fly-fishing.

I said, "The information I need is about a guy named John Reilley. I'd like to know if he has a bank account on the island."

She looked at me, then shook her head. "Would you want a bank to tell people if you had an account there? Then what would be next, your account number?"

"I know there's a way to find out," I said. "I just don't know what it is." I felt a smile on my face. "I take it you're not it."

She smiled back. "Sorry, J.W. I will tell you this, though, just for old times' sake. John Reilley doesn't have an account at Vineyard Haven National. I know who John is, and I've never seen him in here."

"Well, that narrows the field a little, anyway."

"Try some of your shady friends. One of them might know somebody with that sort of information."

"I don't have any shady friends. I only have some friends who don't talk much about what they do."

"Like me, in this case." She laughed and I left.

It was past noon and I was hungry, so I walked through the windy rain down to the E and E Deli for lunch. The boy behind the counter was the same one who'd been there when Paul Fox had gotten himself shot. He gave me a nervous look and an excellent sandwich.

While I ate it I wondered if John Reilley came in here often, and if so, why. Did he live nearby? When I finished the sandwich I went back to the counter and asked the boy if John Reilley was a steady customer.

"Who's John Reilley?" he asked.

I described John and said that he'd been there the day of the shooting. The kid didn't remember him.

I drove to Edgartown, my windshield wipers slapping time just like in "Bobby McGee." I parked right in front of the courthouse and went inside. John Reilley had never been arrested or done anything else to get his name on official records.

Saint John.

I drove to the police station and went into the Chief's office. He was busy with papers. I pointed at his computer. "I thought those things were going to eliminate the need for paper and file cabinets and all that sort of thing."

"Ha! I have more paperwork now than I did before. I have to keep backup records of everything in case the computer goes down. If the damned computer goes down, the whole world stops. You're smart not to have one in spite of what people say about your brain."

I sat down across from him. "I'm trying to find out where John Reilley lives. You ever do any business with him?"

"You're dripping on my floor. I know who John Reilley is. He rides that moped everywhere, summer and winter. But he's never come to our attention, as the papers sometimes say. He must live somewhere, but I don't know where. Doesn't he work for Connell and Carlson, building some of these castles people are putting up nowadays?"

"I guess I'll try to catch him at work."

"That's more than anybody will ever be able to do if they're looking for you. How's the family?"

"The family is fine, including the cats. John Reilley is a hard guy to find."

"I wish I was," said the Chief, giving me a steady look. "People interrupt me here all the time. Please don't tell me that you've got your nose in this Saberfox affair, because we already have some company vigilantes telling us how to do our business. A couple of them know for sure that Rick Black took that shot at Paul Fox and they're mad as wet hens because we haven't already arrested him. They don't think we've even got him on the suspect list. I swear I'm going to quit this job and move to Nova Scotia."

He'd been saying that for years. I left him to his pile of papers and went dripping back out into the wind and rain.

— 9 —

The weather was the kind that kept contractors from doing outside work, so my chances of spotting John Reilley before he spotted me were pretty slim. To find him I'd probably have to go inside whatever mansion he was helping to build and that would tip him off that I was snooping.

So I went home and phoned Connell and Carlson's office.

"I've just bought a piece of property on Edgartown harbor," I said to the woman who answered. "I plan to take the place down and rebuild, and your firm has been recommended to me. If this weather ever clears I'd like to take a look at some of the projects you're working on. Nothing formal, just a look to get an idea about your work. If I like it, I'll get back to you. You have anything being built right now?"

Of course they did, and she told me where. In return, she got my name, Quincy Adams, a fictitious Connecticut phone number (I was only on the island for a couple of days this trip), and my reassurances that if I liked what I saw at the building site I'd be by to talk to someone in the office.

The quicker the better, advised the woman. Business was booming and more orders were coming in all the time. Did I want someone to meet me at the site?

I said no, because my schedule was tight and I didn't know yet when I'd be free, but if she'd advise the foreman that I hoped to come by in the next two days, I'd appreciate it.

She understood perfectly.

The house was being built on a Chilmark hill off Middle Road. I drove through the rain and found the lane leading up to the site. There were other large summer houses along the road, both below and above the new construction. I loafed past the parked pickups of the workmen and the Connell and Carlson trucks and vans and saw that the new house was going to be a beauty, with no expense spared. Just like the place Quincy Adams was going to build in Edgartown.

Better yet, I saw a moped with a box behind the seat leaning against a tree. Clearly a little rain did not stay John Reilley from using his bike to get to and from work.

I turned around in a driveway up the hill from the construction site and drove back. In a driveway near Middle Road I found a place where I could park and wait pretty much out of sight of anyone coming down the hill.

But not today. I had other duties to perform and drove home to do them. By the time the kids came sloshing down the driveway, kicking pools of water as they came, I had warm cocoa and cookies waiting and supper, a seafood casserole, ready for the oven.

I got them out of their rain gear and put them in front of the fire to warm up while they snacked and gave me their reports of their day. School didn't seem to have changed much from when I was a kid their age.

"Pa?"

"What?"

"Can we go out and play in the rain?"

"No, not today. Today you play inside."

"Aw, Pa!"

I pointed to the sign above the kitchen door. "What does that say?"

"'No sniveling.' But we're not sniveling."

"You're getting ready to. No, today is an indoor day. Do you have any homework?"

"No. Can we watch television?"

"What's on?"

"I don't know."

"You can watch for one hour."

As far as I knew, we had the only black-and-white TV on Martha's Vineyard, or maybe in the whole world. Zee and I watched Red Sox games sometimes, so I couldn't argue when Joshua and Diana wanted to watch something for an hour. I didn't care what they watched and rarely had to advise them that their hour was up, since they were usually bored by then.

They had abandoned the tube and the three of us were on the floor playing Crazy Eights by the time Zee came home, shrugged out of her raincoat, and gave her children and me kisses. After she changed into other clothes, she joined us in the game. Crazy Eights is one of those games that can be played just as well by kids as by grown-ups, and is far better entertainment than television. The cats lay on the rug watching us. It was quality family time.

After taking a beating from my children, I left the game, put the casserole in the oven, got the vodka out of the freezer, and filled two glasses. Two olives per glass, black ones for Zee, green ones stuffed with peppers for me, completed the drinks. She, too, then abandoned the game and while we sipped the drinks in front of the fire and watched Joshua and Diana battle it out on the floor, I told her what Maria Donawa had asked me to do and about my day since then.

"Well," said Zee, "I suppose I might want to protect my mother, too. Do you really think John Reilley might be a gigolo or even dangerous?"

"He's never done anything to attract the attention of the local police. People who cause trouble usually do."

"What are you going to do next?"

"I thought I might follow him home tomorrow, just to see where he lives. He has to live somewhere, but nobody knows where. So far, in fact, nobody knows much about him at all."

"But he's been on the island for quite a while, hasn't he? Somebody must know about him. Why don't you just ask him about himself?"

"Dodie asked him where he lives, but when Maria tried to check out the address, she couldn't find it. I don't think Maria wants her mother or him to know she's checking up on him. By tomorrow night I should know where he lives, at least."

"I'll leave work early tomorrow, so I'll be here when the tots get home. That'll give you time to play detective."

I put my arm around her. "What more can a man ask than the love of a good woman?"

"How about the love of a bad one?" she asked, putting a grasping hand in a delicate spot.

"You're right!" I said in falsetto.

"What did you say, Pa?"

"Nothing, Diana."

The next day was cold but clear, and about four in the afternoon I made a fruitless stop at Dodie's house just in case John had stopped by for tea. He hadn't, and a half hour later I was parked in the hidden driveway in Chilmark reading Velikovsky, who had written my car book, and waiting for the work gang to leave the half-built house up the hill.

A dark green Range Rover went up the lane. Was that a Saberfox car, or was it carrying someone else who made more money than most of the carpenters on the job?

Just as I got to the part of Velikovsky's book where the Earth is first brushed by the tail of Venus, vehicles began to come down the lane. I put the book in the door pocket and started my engine.

After a few minutes John Reilley passed by on his moped and I let a pickup go by before easing out behind him. At the foot of the lane John and the pickup turned left and headed for West Tisbury. I trailed along with yet other trucks and cars behind me. The narrow, up-island roads are not conducive to passing, so we wound along head to tail like a mother duck and her ducklings.

In West Tisbury, John and the pickup headed toward Edgartown. That was interesting because John had told Dodie that he lived near the Vineyard Haven–West Tisbury line.

Maybe he was going shopping in Edgartown before he went home.

But instead of going to Edgartown, he turned left on Airport Road and putted along toward the blinker. The pickup that had been between us went straight on, but a line of oncoming cars from Edgartown kept me from turning left and following the moped. When I finally managed it, John was far ahead and there were several cars between us.

That would have been fine, but then one of the cars in front of me was held up by more oncoming traffic before making a left turn into the industrial park. By the time my line of cars got going again, John was out of sight.

Blad dast it! When I'm king of the world I'm banning all left turns.

When I finally got to the blinker John was still out of sight. I had three choices: right to Edgartown, where a cold-looking hitchhiker was trying to thumb a ride, left to Vineyard Haven, or straight ahead to Oak Bluffs. Since John could have gone to either Edgartown or Vineyard Haven by shorter routes than this one, I went toward Oak Bluffs, following Barnes Road.

With me hurrying and John on a moped, I figured I should catch up with him, but John did not come into view.

Hmmmm.

I turned around at the fire department and drove back to the blinker. The hitchhiker was still there, looking colder than ever. I pulled over to him and stopped. He opened the door and got in.

"Thanks, buddy. I thought I was going to freeze my ass off out there."

"The first rule of hitching is that nobody owes you a ride. How long have you been here?"

"Half hour, maybe."

"You see a moped go by, coming from the airport?"

"Nah. Too cold for mopeds. Summer is moped time."

"Where you headed?"

"Edgartown. I got a room there. Got to clear out of it in June, but it's mine for now."

"I'll take you to your door."

"Well, thanks, buddy. I appreciate that."

I drove him to his address, because I owed him that much, then went back to the blinker. Somewhere between there and the industrial park John Reilley had turned off. I turned into the Deer Run development and followed its various streets, seeing no sign of the moped. Then I drove back to Airport Road and drifted slowly along looking for driveways. There weren't too many, but when I found one I took it: houses but no mopeds.

A lot of the land was state forest that contained bicycle paths and fire lanes but few buildings of any kind. Had John driven off on one of those paths? I pulled over and stopped and looked down one as far as I could see.

No John was in sight.

Mysteriouser and mysteriouser.

I checked my rearview mirror to make sure I wouldn't get run over when I pulled back onto the road. Back there a quarter of a mile or so was what looked like a green Range Rover parked by the side of the road.

I drove toward the Edgartown–West Tisbury road. The green Range Rover pulled onto the highway and followed along. I turned toward Edgartown and a bit later saw that the Range Rover had done the same.

I had a tail.

— 10 —

Just to be sure, I turned onto Metcalf Drive, drove a half mile or so, and stopped in front of a house. In jig time the Range Rover came around a corner behind me. It seemed to hesitate, then drove on by. The driver and passenger didn't look at me, but I looked casually at them. They were both wearing ties.

When the car was out of sight, I waited a few minutes, then drove on. Around the next corner I met it coming back. I gave it not a glance because I already had the license plate number and knew what the driver and passenger looked like. The plate was from Georgia.

I wondered how long I'd been followed and why Saberfox was interested in me. The tail could have been there from the time I'd left home and I just hadn't been paying attention. The first time I'd noticed a Range Rover was when I'd seen that one headed up the road to the work site, but maybe that wasn't the occupants' first sight of me.

There's a small traffic circle where Metcalf Drive joins Dodgers Hole Road. I went around the circle and parked facing back toward Metcalf Drive. Sure enough, the Range Rover soon came along. I was fairly sure that its occupants were not pleased to see me waiting for them, but they had little choice but to keep driving. When the car entered the traffic circle I followed after it, the tailed now tailing the tailer.

The car's occupants, sure now that they'd been spotted, sped off ahead of me along Dodgers Hole Road. Their new car could certainly outrun my old one, but there are several speed bumps on Dodgers Hole Road, so they beat up their vehicle a bit as they fled. Some day I'd like a Range Rover of my own, but at that time I took pleasure in the damage they were doing to theirs as I watched them pull away from me. By the time I got to the Vineyard Haven–Edgartown road the Range Rover was not to be seen.

I drove to the State Police barracks and no one followed me. I found Dom Agganis at his desk.

"I'm seeing a lot of you lately," he said. "To what do I owe this particular honor?"

I told him about my day and asked him to verify my guess that the Range Rover belonged to Saberfox. He checked and it did. "You want me to find out why Saberfox is tailing you?" he asked.

"I plan to ask them that myself. I just thought you might want to know it was happening. But you'll be remembered in my will if you can tell me where John Reilley lives. He slipped my noose."

He leaned back. "Why are you looking for John Reilley? I hope you're not nosing around in police business. Like that shooting in Vineyard Haven, for instance."

I put a hand on my heart. "Heaven forbid," I said, and told him about Maria Donawa's concerns.

"Well, that explains your interest in John. Why do you suppose Fox is so interested in you?"

I'd been thinking about that. "He knows where I

live, so I don't think it's me that interests him. My best guess is that he wants me to lead him to somebody else."

He nodded. "Who?"

"I'd think it was John Reilley except that there's no reason for Fox to believe I'd lead him to John. But I don't know who else it could be."

"How many people know you're looking for John?"

"Not too many. Maria Donawa, Zee, Hazel Fine, and a couple of others."

Dom stretched his heavy arms and wiggled his thick fingers in a sort of mini exercise routine. "Well, you know the saying: two can keep a secret if one of them is dead. Maybe one of the ladies told a friend who told a friend and so forth."

"Yeah, it could be. Now, how about telling me where John lives, so I can save myself a lot of time and energy."

Dom put his hands together and cracked his knuckles. It was a talent I did not possess. "I hate to destroy my reputation for omniscience," he said, "but I have to admit that I don't know where John Reilley hangs his hat."

We considered that fact in silence for a while.

"There's a curious lack of information about John," I said finally.

"Indeed," Dom agreed. "Nothing illegal about living a very private life, of course."

"Nothing at all." I stood up. "Anything new on the Kirkland killing or the shot at Paul Fox?"

"The investigations are proceeding, as we say in the police biz."

"Any arrests imminent?"

"When I was a kid I always got *imminent, immanent,* and *eminent* mixed up. That ever happen to you?"

"Constantly. I take it that's a no."

"You take it correctly. Keep in touch. All of this may tie together."

I went home and nobody followed me. I told Zee what I'd told Dom.

"If you want to find out where John Reilley lives," she said, "tomorrow morning go up there where you lost him and park yourself someplace where you can see the road. When he goes to work, you'll see where he comes from."

Smart Zee.

"Unless," she added, "he actually lives somewhere else entirely."

Unless that, of course.

She frowned. "I don't like this business of people following you."

"I don't even like me following John Reilley."

"I don't either, but you're doing Maria a favor. I don't know what those Saberfox guys are up to. You be careful."

Early the next morning I drove back to Airport Road. No one followed me. Maybe I'd embarrassed them into staying home.

I parked the Land Cruiser a hundred yards in on the entrance road that led to the state forest head-quarters, walked back to Airport Road, and found a tree to lean against while I looked up and down the highway and watched early risers drive to wherever they were going. I was chilly and wishing that I'd remembered to bring a jug of coffee with me when I turned my head to look back toward the blinker and saw a moped coming toward me along the highway. I slid behind the tree and watched John Reilley go by, apparently headed back to work in Chilmark.

I waited until he was well down the road, then got into the truck and drove slowly in the direction John had come from. I hadn't see him emerge onto the blacktop, but he hadn't been there just moments before, so I knew about where he had to have come out.

The problem was that there wasn't a road or path where he'd come onto the pavement. I turned around at the blinker and drove back, studying the ground and foliage.

Nothing.

Traffic was picking up as starting times approached for most working people. Unlike them I had no obligation to be anywhere. It was one advantage of not having a real job. A compensating disadvantage was that I also had little money. All in all I preferred the freedom to the cash, as did the hoboes looking for the Big Rock Candy Mountain.

I parked beside the road and walked first on one side, then the other, looking at the ground for spoor as I'd been told the African trackers do when leading game walks and drives and as the American Indians and other hunters no doubt also do.

I'm not Lew Wetzel or Trader Horn or Abraham Mahsimba, but I'm not blind either. I had walked several hundred yards up the road and was coming back when I saw the track of the moped's tires in a small patch of soft earth on the west side of the pavement.

I looked in the direction the track had come from, then walked that way seeing hints of tire marks on the grass. Beyond the first line of trees and scrub oak a paved bike path paralleled the highway. On the other side of the bike path, where the real forest began, there were no tire tracks. Careful John Reilley had apparently driven along the bike path for a while before cutting out to the highway.

I followed the bike path back toward the blinker but saw no sign of a moped track leading from the forest. Returning, I was almost opposite my parked truck when I finally saw where John had come out onto the path. His trail was faint and led from between two pine trees that would have hidden him from the view of anyone on the path or on the highway. John could study the public world for a while and enter it only when there was no one to see him do it.

I looked into the forest. Many of the trees and bushes were still leafless, and I could look deep and see places I could never see in the summertime.

I saw nothing related to human beings: no house, no shed, no half-fallen stone fence. A hundred years before, all this forest had been grassy grazing land for sheep and cattle, where farmers had walked and worked. Now it was wilderness.

I went into the woods, moving slowly through scrub oak and blackjack pine, following what had now become a faint trail of moped tracks through the undergrowth. A hundred yards into the forest I looked back. The seemingly open woods had closed behind me and I could no longer see the highway. I turned and went on.

I came to a lightning-blasted tree. Once large and tall, it was now a charred, splintered stump perhaps twenty feet high. I could almost smell the smoke from that ancient bolt of fire.

Other stumps were in sight, these showing the markings of crosscut saws where loggers now long dead had timbered out the area before the current crop of oak and pine had grown in. On the far side of a small meadow there was what looked like an old cellar hole. I went there and looked down into it. Fallen stones half filled it, the remains of what had once been a foundation, and ancient, warped beams and boards lay tumbled among them. Such old foundations can be found all over the Vineyard, mute testaments to long-forgotten ambitions of island men and women.

The moped tracks led past the hole and into a patch of greenbrier. I had no intention of tangling with greenbrier thorns, so I circumnavigated the patch. No track led out the other side. I got as close to the greenbrier as I cared to, stood on my tiptoes, and stared into its center. There I thought I could see a piece of camouflaged tarp.

John was fond of camouflage. He kept his moped in the Greenbrier Garage. Home must be nearby.

11

There were two ways to find John's lair: I could look for it myself, or I could let him show it to me. I decided on the latter. Tonight when John came to the clearing after work, I'd be watching.

I found my spot to do that fairly quickly, a small, crooked fir not far from the cellar hole with branches that swept the ground, providing a hidden shelter just the right size for me.

No problem.

I circled away from John's path on my way back to the highway, picking up a few scratches as I traveled, but feeling pretty good about my detective work. I fetched the bike path a few hundred yards from my truck and had almost begun to whistle a happy, self-congratulatory tune when I saw the Range Rover.

It was parked behind my truck and a large man with a necktie was doing something at my rear bumper. Another large, necktied man was looking up and down the road and into the trees, his head on a busy swivel. The lookout was not too good at his job and was peering in other directions when I slipped behind a tree trunk and watched the action from there.

The men climbed back into the Range Rover and drove toward me. I eased around the tree trunk as they passed by and watched them pull off onto a side road about a quarter of a mile to the south. The driver and passenger were the same two guys I'd seen the day before. I waited for them to reappear, but they didn't.

After a bit I walked on up the bike path and cut through the underbrush and trees to my truck. Inside my rear bumper was a small electronic device held in place by duct tape. I didn't think it was a bomb because a bomb would have been placed up where the driver sat. A bug to allow someone to follow me, then.

The guys in the Range Rover were apparently waiting for me to leave so they could follow me at a distance without being seen. Maybe they had some sort of modern electronic monitor that showed exactly where I was on a video map. Did such things actually exist, or were they only make-believe gadgets that I had seen in the movies? My ignorance of modern electronics was staggering.

Maybe I should at least break down and buy a computer. As far as I knew, I was the only person in the Western world who didn't have one. Should I get one for the kids, or could they use the ones at school? Problems, problems.

I checked beneath the car and under the hood but found no other devices that hadn't been there before, then climbed in and drove to Vineyard Haven where I parked in the A&P parking lot. The Range Rover was nowhere in sight, but there were a couple of Tisbury police cruisers parked in front of the impressive new police station across from the grocery store.

For several years Edgartown had held the championship for the snazziest police station on the Vineyard, but now it had stiff competition from both

Vineyard Haven and Chilmark, where the old coast guard station has become the new police station. Time rolls on, in spite of the efforts of many monied islanders to make it stop or go backward.

Nobody seemed to be paying any attention to me, so I got a roll of duct tape from the back of the truck, cut the tape holding the tracking device, and went over to one of the cruisers. Still, nobody was giving me heed. Where are the cops when you really need them? I taped the gadget to the inside of the cruiser's rear bumper and went back to my truck. I wondered how long it would take the guys in the Range Rover to realize that they were tailing a police car.

How would they feel when they found out? How would their boss feel?

I drove to the hospital and found Zee and another nurse at the desk of the emergency room, doing paperwork. Zee seemed happy to see me and returned the kiss I gave her.

"What brings you here, hunk?"

"An emergency. I thought my heart would stop beating if I had to stay away from you a moment longer."

"Good grief," said the other nurse.

"He's always like this," said Zee. "He can't live without me. Can you, dear?"

"An eternity in hell would be bliss compared to an hour without you, my sweet."

"Ye gods!" said the nurse. "I'll leave you two alone." She walked away.

"How's your gudgeon?" I asked.

"Fine. How's your pintle?"

"My pintle is okay, I'm glad to tell you."

"And I'm happy to hear it. Now, why are you really here?"

"Two things. I need to be free a little after four. Can you shake loose from here early again today?" I told her about finding John Reilley's trail.

She nodded. "I can probably leave early. It's been a slow day. What's the other thing?"

"I'm going to talk with Donald Fox. Paul Fox was in here after he got shot, so I figured you have big brother's local address and phone number somewhere in your files."

She went away and came back with a slip of paper in her hand. "You figured right. Apparently, Saberfox has taken over the whole Martin's Vineyard Hotel, right here in town. Their office is there, and so are the living quarters for the entire high command: the Fox brothers and Brad Hillborough. Why do you want to see Donald Fox?"

"I want to know why those guys were tailing me. They were there again today."

She picked up on the tense. "Were?"

"I think the dogs may be chasing a red herring at the moment, but they'll be back. I'd like to know why. While I'm asking questions, do you know if Paul Fox is still on the island? Donald wanted him to go home to Savannah, but Paul didn't seem anxious to leave."

"And he didn't. Maria tells me that he and she and his cracked ribs went to the movies night before last. Apparently Donald's wish is not Paul's command. Are you sure you want to get more involved in whatever it is that's going on?"

"I'm already involved. I may have to get more involved in order to get uninvolved."

The Martin's Vineyard Hotel is a couple of streets in back of Ocean Park, and was built in the time when an ocean view was not held in such high esteem as it is nowadays. It's a big old Victorian place with wide porches and a lot of gingerbread decoration. It's well maintained and is painted in four different colors, as are many of the cottages around the campground because, I've been told, that was the way the buildings were painted back in the 1800s, when the places were new.

The name comes from early maps, some of which identify the island as Martin's Vineyard while others call it Martha's Vineyard. Bartholomew Gosnold, who named the island in 1602, could have used either name since his mother-in-law, who helped finance his voyage, was named Martha, since he supposedly had a daughter by that name, and since John Martin was the captain of one of Gosnold's ships.

In any event, Martha eventually overcame Martin and got the island for herself, leaving Martin with only a Victorian hotel. The hotel was probably glad to have Saberfox's business during the winter, when there were few other customers about. Maybe Saberfox paid so well that the company would be welcome all summer, too.

I didn't know if Donald Fox would be there in midmorning, but I also didn't know he wouldn't be, so I went in. A clerk came out from an office behind the desk, and looked more than slightly surprised at having a customer who didn't work for Saberfox. She instantly knew I didn't because I wasn't wearing a suit and tie. She recovered nicely and smiled and asked if she could help me. I told her I wanted to see

Donald Fox. She told me I could find the Saberfox office on the second floor and pointed to a graceful staircase across the lobby.

I crossed the room, taking in the decor as I went. The walls were hung with paintings and photos of square-rigged ships and Victorian scenes. Art nouveau statues and vases stood on tables, and ornately carved chairs and couches lined the sides of the room. Colored light filtered through stained-glass windows beside and over the door and brightened the worn but still lovely Oriental carpets on the floor. There was a faint smell of lavender in the air.

I went up the worn stairs and found myself in another lobby. A woman sat at a large desk upon which was a computer and a small sign that read SABERFOX, INC. Facing the desk were two comfortable chairs. On a table between the chairs were a half dozen magazines. They appeared to be the latest issues. Clearly I wasn't in a doctor's office. The woman was wearing a suit and a necktie. What else?

"I'm Dana Hvide," she said. "What can I do for you?"

I told her I'd like to speak with Donald Fox.

Her eyes flowed over my clothing. Clearly I wasn't the type who normally had access to Donald Fox.

"I'm afraid Mr. Fox is busy this morning, Mr. . . . ?"

"Jackson." I gave her my best smile. It was like smiling at a rock.

"As I said, I'm afraid Mr. Fox is busy this afternoon, Mr. Jackson." She fingered her keyboard and looked at her computer screen. Whatever happened to appointment books? "Mr. Fox's assistant, Mr. Jacobs, may be able to help you."

"I doubt it. Perhaps you can tell Mr. Fox that J. W.

Jackson would like to talk with him. I think he'll want to see me, and I won't need much of his time."

"As I just told you, Mr. Jackson, Mr. Fox is busy. He can't be interrupted."

"Anybody can be interrupted," I said. "Work can be interrupted, too, and jobs. Yours, for instance, might be if you don't tell your boss that I'm here. I think he'll be annoyed if you don't do that."

Her eyes hardened. "Mr. Fox's work is very important. He takes it very seriously." She leaned forward. "And I take mine seriously. Don't try to threaten me!"

I admired her. What is more valuable to a businessman than a loyal secretary who will defend you from your enemies?

"The graveyards are full of indispensable people," I said. "I'll wait."

I sat down and picked up a magazine. It had to do with country living. I more or less lived in the country, so I began to read. The country it described was another country than mine.

After a few minutes Dana Hvide picked up a phone and spoke into it. I heard my name mentioned. She listened and said, "Certainly, sir," and put the phone down. She stood and gestured toward a door. "Please go right in, Mr. Jackson."

I went in.

12

Fox was standing behind his desk when I came in. Brad Hillborough was leaning on his cane beside a chair off to one side. In front of Fox, seated in chairs, were two other men. Everybody was wearing a suit and tie and looking at me.

At the far side of the room was a conference table. On the wall beyond it was a gigantic map of Martha's Vineyard. The small, colored flags stuck in the map reminded me of those used in maps in military operation centers: Here is the enemy, here is us, here is where we want to be; we're gathered together to discuss how to get there. When the discussion is over, I will decide what to do and you will go do it.

"Well, well, Mr. Jackson," said Fox, "have you changed your mind about working with us?"

"No. I just have a question." I glanced at the two men in the chairs.

"These are trusted colleagues, Mr. Jackson," said Fox. "You can speak freely. Allow me to introduce them. Gentlemen, this is Mr. J. W. Jackson, of whom I have spoken. Mr. Jackson, this is Jonathan Burns and this is Samuel Jacobs."

The men rose and put temporary smiles on their otherwise emotionless faces. As we shook hands and exchanged assurances that our meeting was a pleasure, they studied me with their entrepreneurial eyes.

"Now, Mr. Jackson, what is it you wish to know?" Fox glanced at his watch. Time is money.

"Yesterday," I said, "two men in a green Range Rover with Georgia plates followed me until they realized that I'd spotted them and broke off their surveillance. Today, when they thought I wasn't looking, they put a tracking device on my car to make their job easier. I got a good look at the men before I got rid of the tracking device."

Fox's eyes seemed to brighten. They moved to Jacobs and Burns and came back to me.

"My question is: Why are they doing it? I thought it might save us all a lot of time if you just told me what you want to know."

Fox stared at me. "Are you sure of your facts?"

I nodded. "I switched the tracking device to a Tisbury police cruiser, so your two boys will be following the cops instead of me for a while, at least. I thought I'd use the time to have this chat with you. So, what is it that you think you'll learn by following me around?"

Fox looked silently at me. Then he said, "You're absolutely sure of what you're saying? You're not mistaken about anything you've told me?"

"I'm sure. Dom Agganis checked the car's owner-ship. It's one of yours. I'm curious about your inter-est in my travels."

"I have no interest in your travels, Mr. Jackson." He turned and looked again at Jacobs and Burns. "Do either of you know what this is about?" His voice was cold.

They seemed almost to squirm before his gaze. They flicked glances at each other beneath raised brows and shook their heads, then looked back at

Fox and shook them some more. "I don't know anything about it, Donald," said Burns.

"It's news to me," agreed Jacobs with a nervous shrug.

"Nothing that our people do should be news to you two," snapped Fox. "First someone tries to kill my brother, then Kirkland is murdered, and now this! And you two know nothing about any of it!"

Jacobs appeared to shrink in size. Burns was cooler. He looked at me. "Please describe the two men, Mr. Jackson, and provide me with the license number of the vehicle, if you have it."

I did that. Burns frowned. "Sounds like Wall and Reston," he said. "If you'll excuse me, Donald, I'll get right on this."

"You do that," said Fox in a voice like ice. "And you go with him, Sam. Try to do something right for a change!"

"Yes, Donald!" Jacobs scurried after the departing Burns.

Fox took a deep breath, sat down, and waved at a chair. "Please sit down, Mr. Jackson. I'm again in your debt, it seems. I hope you'll believe me when I tell you that this surveillance you've experienced was not authorized by me."

I decided not to come to any conclusion about that, but I took the chair and nodded. "When you figure this business out," I said, "I'd like to know what's going on."

"I intend to find out. And when I do—" He broke off his speech and his mouth became a hard line across his face.

"And when you do, you might tell me about it if it doesn't interfere with business."

He inclined his head slightly. "Knowledge is power. When I know the truth of this matter, I'll decide what information to share." He put the tips of his long fingers together. "Does it offend you that I might decline to give you information after I've willingly accepted information from you?"

"No. You owe me nothing. I'm not interested in the kind of power you value."

He studied me. "What other kind is there?"

"You'll get more from a book on philosophy than from me. There's power over other people and there's power over yourself. I'm not good at the second kind, but I work at it because it interests me; the first kind doesn't."

His voice was cynical. "The second is only a tool to achieve the first."

I said nothing.

He sat back, his eyes aglow, perhaps with anger. Then he seemed to will his ire away. In a neutral voice, he asked, "What do you make of this surveillance business? Why do you think you were being followed?"

"Maybe some loyal operatives of yours think I know somebody or something that you should know."

"What, for instance?"

I shook my head. "I came here hoping you could tell me."

"But perhaps you do know someone or something that I should know. Do you, Mr. Jackson?"

Beyond Fox I could see Brad Hillborough looking at me with interest, his head cocked slightly to one side.

"I can't imagine who or what that might be," I

said, "but maybe you've got some enemy action on your hands."

Fox stared at me with thoughtful eyes.

"And," I said, "maybe the enemy's living in your house."

"What do you mean? Why do you say that?"

Brad Hillborough answered. "He says it because the surveillance team consists of Saberfox people."

I nodded. "That's right. You seem to have a company problem, Mr. Fox. People under your roof are doing things you don't know about."

Fox's face was grim. "Not for much longer. I've left too much of my business in the hands of people who apparently can't be trusted. My brother has been urging me to give him more responsibility. Maybe the time has come to do that." He stood up. "Are you sure you won't work for me?"

"I'm sure."

"Then I'll simply thank you for bringing this matter to my attention. If you'll excuse me now, I have work to do."

I stood and Brad Hillborough did the same. "I'll escort Mr. Jackson to his car," he said.

We went out past the desk and down to the main lobby. Brad Hillborough limped along silently until we were outside, standing by my old Land Cruiser. Then he looked around the parking lot and said, "You're in the middle of this somehow. Want to tell me about it?"

"Like I said upstairs, I came here so your boss could explain things to me. If I knew what was going on, I wouldn't have needed to ask."

"If you know more than you're telling me and I find out about it, I'll take it amiss."

I felt my eyelids lower slightly. "Fox is lucky to have somebody like you on his side," I said. "That cane tells me how loyal you are. Tell me about Albert Kirkland. Why do you think he got himself killed?"

"Albert was a hardworking fellow," said Hillborough, "but Donald trusted him."

"Did you?"

He hesitated, then said, "I brought him into the company. Donald hired him on my recommendation."

"Did Kirkland like to have a few at the local bars?"

Hillborough shook his head. "He didn't drink at all. I believe he was meeting someone in the last place anybody would expect him to be. I wish I knew who. The police haven't told us much more than's in the papers."

"They don't know everything. Do you know anyone working for the company who drinks at the Fireside tavern?"

He studied me, then shook his head. "I had a beer there when we first came to the island. I haven't been back since. It's not my kind of place. If any of our people have been there, I've not heard about it. Why?"

"Because a man who may have been Kirkland met somebody driving a green Range Rover in that parking lot a couple of days before Paul Fox got shot and Kirkland got killed."

Hillborough rubbed his chin. "Is that a fact? Well, well."

"Another question: Do you know anybody in the Saberfox crew who carries a long-bladed knife and knows how to use it?"

He smiled wryly. "We've talked about that in the office. Donald likes to hire fencers. We have several working for us, including Paul and me, although none of us was ever in Donald's league. Even Al Kirkland could fence well enough to try out for the pentathlon team, although he never made it."

"Were any of your other fencers mad at Kirkland? How about your boss, for instance?"

Hillborough's face darkened and he lifted his silver-headed cane and shook it at me. "You watch what you say about Donald, you hear me? I'll have no one speak ill of him. No one!" He leaned forward, his eyes wildly bright. "And if you try to harm him in any way, I'll make you sorry you were ever born!"

I looked down at the cane and after a moment he took it away. I got into the truck and left. As I drove I looked in my rearview mirror. He was still standing there, watching me, like some angry, lame berserker.

13

After Zee got home that afternoon I drove back to Airport Road, tucked the Land Cruiser out of sight, well away from the entrance to John Reilley's lair, and walked into the woods, taking a roundabout path to the site.

The hiding place under the crooked little fir was just right for my purposes. I could see out, but it would be hard for anyone to spot me. I arranged myself as comfortably as possible and got out my paperback car book. I didn't have a lot of reading light, but there was no use in wasting what I had.

Velikovsky was comparing some Mayan myths to Old Testament stories about earthly disasters when I heard the distant sound of a small engine from the direction of the road. Then the sound stopped. I put away my book, and a few minutes later heard someone coming along the little path I'd found earlier in the day.

I peeked out and John Reilley, pushing his moped, came into view. He paused and looked casually around. His eyes passed over my hiding place and moved on. Then he pushed the moped across to the patch of greenbrier, parted some of the vines, and entered it by some route I'd missed. I watched him cover the moped with the tarp. Then he came out of the briers, gave another offhand look at the forest around him, and disappeared into the cellar hole.

I was surprised by how quickly it happened. In one moment he was standing there, glancing around, and in the next he was gone.

I waited for him to reappear, but he did not, so after a few minutes I crawled out of my spy nest and walked to the cellar hole. It looked exactly as it had before, half filled with a jumble of stones and rotting wood. There was no sign of John.

I sat on my heels and studied the site. Leaning haphazardly against the far wall was a pile of broken and apparently rotting boards and timbers, seemingly the collapsed remains of what had once been the floor of the long-disappeared building above the cellar hole.

John had to have gone somewhere, and there was nowhere else he could have gone. Since, as Holmes observed, when all other possibilities have been eliminated, what remains must be true, John had gone behind that pile of lumber.

I climbed down and crossed to the jumble of rotten pieces of wood.

It was not, of course, a jumble of rotten pieces of wood but a carefully constructed doorway made to look like a jumble of rotten pieces of wood. When I looked where I figured there had to be hinges, there were hinges. When I looked harder I found what served as a door latch. I tried it. Nothing moved. Locked from the inside, certainly.

I put an ear to the door. I could hear nothing. I knocked.

Nothing.

I knocked again, harder this time. After a while I

heard a slight noise above my head and looked up in time to see a hole close in a beam above the doorway. I waited, then knocked a third time. Finally I heard a slight noise from the other side of the door. I stepped back. The peephole quickly opened and shut once again. Then, silently, the door latch turned and the door swung open.

John Reilley stood there, looking out at me. His expression was one of resignation.

"Well," he said. "I guess it was bound to happen sooner or later. Are there more of you?"

"Just me," I said.

He looked beyond me and, seeing no one else, he nodded. "No matter," he said, "one tongue is enough."

"Only if it flaps," I said. "Are you going to invite me in?"

"Why not? Come in, J.W. Shut the door behind you, if you will." He turned and led me down a short, low hallway and into a small room lit by electric lamps. A bunk bed was against one wall and a table and chair against another. A doorway led to another room in which I could see a camp stove and some storage shelves. The walls and the ceiling of the cave were made of lumber scraps of various widths. He sat on the bunk and waved to the chair. "Sit there. I have only that single chair because I never have guests. Until now, that is."

I sat down and looked about me. "Nice," I said. "Cool in the summer, warm in the winter. Where do you get your electricity?"

He seemed willing to talk about his underground house. "There's a construction company just off the Vineyard Haven–Edgartown road. I've tapped into their line. They don't notice what little I use. I get fresh air from a pipe I ran up inside that tall stump you probably noticed. I've got a chemical toilet and I bring in water for cooking. I use the Laundromat for my clothes and I sneak showers after work in the houses I help to build. There aren't many public rest rooms on this island, but I know where every one of them is and I use them to keep clean between showers. I get my books from yard sales and the libraries and I have a TV and radio. The antennas are in trees. You can see them if you know where to look."

"I didn't notice them. How long did it take you to build this place?"

"Three years, and it would have taken longer if I hadn't been able to borrow a pickup to haul the wood I needed. When I started, I was living in Vineyard Haven in an apartment that I had to be out of by summer, so I spent all my free hours that winter digging this first room and lining it with timber so it wouldn't collapse. It was hard work, especially hauling those two-by-tens I used for the ceiling, but by spring I could live here. I enlarged it for a couple of more years until I figured I had as much room as I needed."

"You scatter the dirt out there in the woods?"

He nodded. "It took a lot of time and effort. I'd fill a gunnysack and haul it off and spread the dirt thin, then come back and do it again. I don't recommend it as a way to build yourself a house. You want some coffee? I'm about to brew some."

"Sure."

He went into his kitchen and soon the smell of fresh coffee filled the air. He came back with two cups.

I took mine and said, "I'd guess that one problem was hauling the wood and other stuff in here without being seen. There's a lot of traffic out there on Airport Road."

He nodded. "It was easier in the winter because there weren't so many people around. I couldn't do much in the summer unless I waited till late at night when the moon was bright and I could move through the woods without killing myself. It was slow going. I did better off-season." He sipped his coffee and looked around the room. "And now that the place is finally in shape, here you are and I'll be moving along."

"Not necessarily," I said. "I'm guessing that you must have used that Vineyard Haven apartment to get your PO box and any other papers that required a street address."

"That's right. Once I got the papers, all I needed was the PO box. How'd you know I lived in that apartment?"

"Because I went to the apartment looking for you. I got the address from a friend."

He looked down into the coffee cup. "Are you some kind of cop, J.W.? Why were you looking for me?"

"I'm not a cop. Somebody asked me to find you, that's all."

"Who? Why?"

"I may tell you later, after we talk some more."

"How'd you find me, anyway?"

I told him and he shook his head. "It serves me right. I've been careless lately. Too cocky, too casual. A year ago I would have been watching my back. A year ago you wouldn't have found that tire track."

"I wouldn't have found the track today if I hadn't been looking for it, but you're probably right about getting too sure of yourself. It's pretty common for people who drop out of sight to be very careful at first but then begin to make mistakes as they relax. I think you'd better pay more attention to your security if you plan to keep living here."

He brightened, but it was a careful brightening. "You mean to say you don't plan to spill my beans?"

"I didn't take this job to blab about where you live. I took it to find out something about you."

He sipped his coffee and studied me.

"You're sure you're not some kind of cop?"

"I used to be on the Boston PD, but that was a long time ago. Now I live here and I'm no kind of cop, but you're a mystery somebody wants solved, and I got talked into trying to be the solver."

The brightening in his face went away. "What do you want to know?"

"You might start by telling me why you live here instead of in a house like everybody else."

"I'm antisocial." His stare was steady and he didn't smile.

"You're not so antisocial that you don't get along well with the people you work with, and you're not so antisocial that you don't visit your friends."

He raised a brow. "Like who?"

"Like Dodie Donawa, for one."

"Ah," he said, nodding slowly. "So that's what this is about. Dodie Donawa." He smiled a small, crooked smile.

"It's about Maria, actually," I said. "She doesn't want her mother hurt. She likes you but she doesn't know enough about you to trust her mother to you."

The smile stayed. "Role reversal, eh? Daughters, lock up your mothers; the Vietnam vets are in town for their convention."

"Something like that. And there's another thing."

"What?"

"For the past couple of days two guys who work for Saberfox have been tailing me. It's occurred to me that they may be doing it because I might lead them to someone else whom they can't find. It's also occurred to me that that someone might be you."

The smile fled from his face. "Do you know their names?"

"Wall and Reston. Ring any bells?"

He drank the last of his coffee and held the empty cup in both hands. "You sure they're not cops?"

"Like I said, they work for Saberfox. This is the second or third time you've been worried about the cops. If you're worried about the cops, maybe Maria Donawa is right to be worried about you." He said nothing, but only looked thoughtful and sad. I pushed on. "What's your concern with the police? Are the cops the reason you live in this cave?"

He nodded. "Yes." Then he seemed to come to some agreement with himself. He looked at me. "Forty years ago I killed a man."

— 14 —

There are killings and there are killings, and they're not all the same. I should know.

"Do you want to tell me about it?" I asked.

"You don't look shocked."

"No."

"Another coffee?"

"Sure."

When he came back from the kitchen, he began: "It was a long time ago. There was a woman. The man and I were full of piss and vinegar. All of us were young. The man and I fought what some thought was a fair fight, though I knew it wasn't. Afterward the woman held his body, not me, in her arms. I ran before the police got there. I became John Reilley."

When I said nothing, he went on. He seemed glad to talk.

"I had good hands, so I became a carpenter. It was a kind of work far removed from what I'd done before the killing, and I chose it in part so people who knew me before would probably never meet me. I grew this mustache. Not too big and not too small. Just enough to change my face a little. I've been careful to be friendly but not too friendly, and I always live alone. I want people to like me in a casual way, but not get so close that they'll pry into my background.

"I never stayed anywhere for long until I came here, but even here I didn't want to be too much in the public eye. I had too little money to buy a house, and I didn't want anyone, bank or credit company, for instance, checking into John Reilley's past.

"But I took to the Vineyard. It's beautiful and it's got a population that makes it easy to get lost: a few thousand people in the winter, a hundred thousand during the summer. People coming and going all the time. There's a lot of the kind of work I do and the money's good and people don't ask too many questions as long as you do your job. Everything is in flux, like it is out in northern California, where people are all from somewhere else and probably won't be doing what they're doing now for very long."

"I've never been to northern California."

"Pretty country. Lots of energy in the air. I was there before I came here, and I came here because it was as far from there as I could get and was a place I'd never been. I liked the island, so I rented that apartment and stayed in it long enough to get John Reilley a post office box and to start building this place. I've been here ever since, and somewhere along the line I realized I was tired of moving. Then I met Dodie and was even surer of that. I'm sixty years old, and for forty years I've been on the run. The only women I've known have been the touch-and-go kind. I want to settle down, but I guess that may not happen now that you're here. I'll be moving on if the police don't nail me first."

His face had a fatalistic look that made me uncomfortable. "I told you I don't work for the police," I said, "and I told you I'm not interested in where you live. I just want to know the kind of person you are.

Or rather, Maria Donawa wants to know. How'd you meet Dodie?"

He made a small gesture. "Our lives are a series of happenstance events. Rick Black was dating Maria. Rick and I had worked together on a few jobs. One day after work we bumped into each other in the A&P. I was about to move on when Dodie and Maria came by, and Dodie and I got introduced. If I'd left a half minute sooner we'd never have met. Do you believe in fate?"

The Moirai and Norns seemed as active as ever, but I just shrugged and said, "You and Dodie began to date."

He shook his head. "No. I liked her but I didn't have a place for a woman in my life. Then I met her again at the farmers' market and we talked. It was easy for both of us, but naturally I had to dance around some of her questions."

"I can imagine."

"Then one day Rick told me that Dodie had a small bit of work to do on her porch. He'd promised Maria that he'd take care of it, but he'd gotten a big job that kept him busy and he asked me to stand in for him. I said sure and that was the first time I went to her house. There wasn't much to the job, but afterward she gave me tea and cookies. That was how it started."

"You hit it off."

"Yes." He gave me a challenging look. "Of course she doesn't know that I killed a man."

"Did you ever go back to where that happened?"

"No. I didn't want to disgrace my family, and the woman involved cared about the other man, not me, so I never went back and I never wrote to anyone. By now they must think I'm dead or in prison. I went as far away as my money would take me, changed my name, and got a job. Now I'm here and you know what Maria asked you to learn."

We sat in silence for a while. Then I said, "I've broken all of the commandments at one time or another, so I'm not in a position to judge the fight you had when you were young. I'm only interested in the way you are now, and I'm only interested in that because I know Dodie and I want her to be happy."

"Well," he said, "for what it's worth, in the last forty years John Reilley has never been in trouble, not anywhere for any reason. When it looks like trouble, I fade away. I'm antitrouble. Dodie makes me happy and I think I do the same for her. I'm healthy and I earn a good living and I'm tired of wandering. I'd like to settle down for good."

"What can you tell me about Wall and Reston, the two guys who've been following me? I think they might actually be interested in finding you. Why might that be?"

His eyes narrowed and he shook his head. "I don't know. I don't like it. I've never had people come looking for me before. First you, now maybe these guys Wall and Reston."

"You don't know either one of them?"

"No."

"Homicide cases are never terminated until someone is caught and found guilty. If that killing you were involved with was called murder, the case might be cold but it's not closed. Have you seen anybody on the island who knew you back then and might have recognized you here?"

"No. For forty years I've been looking at faces, but I've never seen one from those days."

"And you haven't written to anybody or told anybody where you are."

"Not in all that time. But here you are and here they are." He rubbed his hand over his head and looked around the room. "I'd better be moving on. Damn!"

"Don't be in too much of a hurry," I said. "Wall and Reston don't know where you are and they may not be after you at all. If they are, it probably has nothing to do with what happened forty years ago. More likely it's something that happened right here."

"Like what?"

"Like you were in the deli when Donald Fox and his men came in, and you went out before they did."

"So what?"

"So you knew he was there and had time to get your pistol and shoot at him."

He threw up his hands. "I don't own a pistol. And why would I try to kill him?"

"I don't know. Maybe because he's trying to take Dodie's house away from her. What matters is what Fox's people may think. Fox says that he doesn't know anything about these guys tailing me, but maybe the two of them figure they'll get in good with the boss if they find the guy who shot his brother, and you're their prime suspect."

He studied me, then shook his head. "No. It's got to be more than that. If they wanted to find me, they could have come to where I've been working. People don't know where I live, but a lot of them know where I am when I'm on a job." He made a small, circular gesture with his forefinger then moved that hand across his chest from right to left as he thought. "It's something else," he said.

"Like what?" I asked. But he only shook his head, so I went on. "Do you know a man named Kirkland?"

A wary look appeared on his face. "I've heard of him. What about him?"

"He's dead. He got himself stabbed in the parking lot behind the Fireside bar in Oak Bluffs."

"Yeah, I read about that in the paper."

"He was probably in the same parking lot a day or so before. He was in a Range Rover like the Saberfox people drive. You ever drive a Range Rover?"

He slowed his words, as though to keep better control of them. "I don't drive a car. I decided it was dangerous to go through the process of getting a license."

I watched him carefully. "I've been wondering if Wall and Reston might be working on something having to do with Kirkland."

He shook his head, but kept his eyes on mine. "I can't imagine a connection with me."

"Dom Agganis asked me if I killed Kirkland. If I'm on Dom's list, even his long list, you probably are, too. And Agganis thinks the shooting and the stabbing are related. So do I, and maybe Wall and Reston do, too. They may even think that you and I are in cahoots."

"But we're not, so why would they think that?"

"We were both there at the deli. You went out and a few minutes later Paul Fox gets shot. I don't say it has to make sense, but people think senseless thoughts all the time." I set my cup aside and stood up. "Thanks for the coffee. Nice place you've got here. I can find my way out."

At the doorway, he touched my arm. "I always use the peephole first, just in case somebody's looking down into the cellar hole. So far nobody ever has been."

I slid a bit of wood aside and looked out. Nothing. I opened the door and went outside.

"What are you going to tell Maria?" he asked.

"I'll give her a report if I ever manage to catch up with you and ask you some questions. Meanwhile, all I can tell her is that you seem to be a steady worker and that the cops don't have your name on any of their lists."

He inclined his head slightly. "Thanks."

"Remember to be more careful with your tracks. If I could find you, maybe Wall and Reston can, too."

"I've learned my lesson." He smiled wryly.

I made a large circle through the forest before emerging onto the bike path beside the road. A slow check of the highway revealed no green Range Rover or other vehicle in sight. I got to the Land Cruiser and drove to Dodie Donawa's house.

— 15 —

My father used to sing about a girl who was "round and firm and fully packed." Dodie Donawa fit that description well. Like her daughter, she was bright, blonde, fair-skinned, and cheerful. I could see why John Reilley might be taken by her and she by him, and could imagine them having a fine time together as they shared the last half of their lives.

If, that is, John was the man he appeared to be when I'd talked with him. Before I reported to Maria, I wanted Dodie's take on John. I don't normally have a lot of faith in intuition, but Jung thought highly of it and I thought highly of Jung. Besides, there's the cliché that women are intuitive, and I'm as good at clichés as the next guy, so I knocked on Dodie's door.

"Why, J.W.," she said, "what brings you here?"

"John Reilley," I said.

Her blue eyes widened. "Are you playing John Alden?"

"No. Sorry."

"Well, come in and enlighten me."

Her living room was furnished with soft, comfortable chairs and a couch facing a television set. There were doilies on the arms of the chair and couch, and in the next room I could see a baby grand piano.

From another room came the sound of Baroque

music, something repetitive enough to be Bach, who often seemed to have done his creating on automatic pilot. But what can you expect from a guy who was probably so busy thinking about his twenty-two children that he often forgot that he'd been writing a particular piece of music a quarter of an hour too long?

Dodie waved me into a chair and plumped herself down on the couch. "Now, what about John?"

"Somebody asked me about him and all I knew was that he seems to be a nice guy and a good worker, and that he rides a moped. I'm hoping you can tell me more about him."

"Who wants to know?"

"Dom Agganis, among others. You know Dom? Sergeant of the State Police. You probably met him when you got caught toting your hog leg into the hospital."

"I know him, but I never even knew that pistol was in my pocket!"

"You've convinced me," I said. "Anyway, John was in the area when somebody shot Paul Fox up at the five corners, and Dom is interviewing people who were there. He's already talked to me, for instance."

"If you ask me, it's too bad the man missed! That Donald Fox is a nasty man and his brother is just as bad. Coming around here like he does, drooling over Maria! Who does he think he is? I wish they'd all go back to wherever it is they came from."

"A lot of people probably agree with you about that, but—"

"That Paul Fox broke up my Maria and that nice Rick Black, you know. I thought Rick and Maria might get married, then along comes that Paul Fox and the first thing you know, he's going off with her! I don't like it! Rick looked after her like a mother hen, but this Fox boy just waltzes her around like she's a beauty queen."

"Maria is a grown woman, Dodie. She—"

"Oh, she's old enough to know better, but she's behaving like a schoolgirl! Won't listen to a word I have to say!"

I managed to get the conversation back on the subject that interested me. "What can you tell me about John Reilley, Dodie? I'll listen to whatever you have to say about him."

She took a deep breath and put her troublesome daughter to one side for the moment. She smiled. "John is wonderful. He and I can talk for hours. Or we can just sit and have a cup of coffee and listen to music or watch TV. He always uses that cup right over there." She pointed at a mug on a sideboard. "Says he likes it. And he likes the same shows that I do."

"He ever tell you what brought him to the Vineyard?"

"He said he came because he'd never been here, but now that he's here he wants to stay." She leaned forward. "If he'll just pop the question, I don't see why he and I can't live right here in the house." Then she frowned. "If that blasted Donald Fox doesn't steal it out from under me, that is!"

"Where was John living before he came here?"

"What?" Dodie came back from angry thoughts of Donald Fox. "Oh. He was out in California. Up north of San Francisco in a place called Inverness. You know, like the city in Scotland. I looked it up in my atlas. He says it's a beautiful place, but the Vineyard is just as pretty."

"I think you may have something to do with him thinking that, Dodie."

Dodie blushed.

"I've talked with John a few times," I said. "I hear some kind of an accent in his voice, but I can't make it out. Where's he from originally, do you know?"

She frowned. "Now that you mention it, I don't think he ever said just where he grew up. But I think what you hear is a teeny bit of Southern drawl in his voice. When I was a girl, I had an aunt down in Louisiana and I used to visit her now and then. When I came home again, my friends would make fun of me because I was talking Southern myself without even realizing it. It's easy to do, you know; you jus' relax yo' mouth lak this." We both laughed.

"I think you're right," I said. "I think that is a trace of Southern I hear when John talks. Not much, but a little. Maybe a little something else, too. Some little accent I can't quite identify. He ever mention his family?"

"Gracious, J.W., you're beginning to make me wonder if I know anything about him at all! He and I are so easy together that I never noticed that he wasn't telling me things like that. Probably because I told him so much that he didn't have a chance!"

"Or maybe he just never thought it was important. And maybe it isn't. I know it isn't important to me what sort of life Zee had before I met her. When we decided to marry, we started from there and we don't talk much about what happened before. It was a different time and we were different people. Does John hunt or fish?"

"He doesn't hunt, but he goes fishing sometimes. And sometimes he and I go clamming on my license.

I tell him to get his own permit because he's a senior citizen and it's free, but I don't think he's done it yet.

"But he sure knows how to cook what we catch. He's at least as good a cook as I am. Says he learned because he didn't want to be one of those guys who ate cold beans. He likes that New Orleans style, and it makes me drool just thinking about it. You like to cook, J.W.?"

I nodded. "I learned for pretty much the same reason. Before I got married I used to cook for myself as though I was going to have company, so I wouldn't get in the habit of eating out of cans just because I was alone. Does John have any favorite dishes he likes to make?"

"He makes wicked-good red beans and rice, and his gumbo beats the band. He's made a Cajun fan out of me, for sure. And he always dries the dishes afterwards. I wash and he dries. It's nice to have a man do that."

Dodie had the form of one who loves to eat. I didn't think she'd lost any weight since John Reilley had come into her life.

I also didn't think she could tell me much more about John than she'd already told. The most important things to her were that he could cook and talk and was wonderful. Maybe that was all that was important. I was more interested in her verification of the slight echoes of a Southern accent in his voice and in what she'd said about his fondness for New Orleans food.

I got up and thanked her and went to the door. On the porch, I turned and said, "I'd like to talk with Maria. Will you have her give me a call when she gets in?"

"I certainly will. But I'm sure she feels the same way about John as I do."

"I'm sure she does. One more thing. Has John ever said anything about Donald Fox?"

Her smile went away. "Only that it'll be a cold day in hell before Fox gets his hands on my house!"

"He said that, did he?"

She nodded. "And I think he meant it, too." She leaned forward. "I like a masterful man, you know what I mean?"

"All of us masterful men appreciate those feelings in our women," I said.

"Oh, you! Be on your way!" She laughed and shut the door.

I was at the end of the walk when a man stepped in front of me. His clothes were those of a working guy, and there was sawdust on his shoes. He was lean and muscular and had an angry look in his eye.

"I know you. You're Jackson. You're the latest Romeo!"

His tone was that of a man looking for trouble.

I said, "What are you talking about?"

He thrust out a sharp chin. "She went to your place. I followed her. Your name's on your mailbox. Don't lie to me, you dirty old man."

I wondered what burr was under his saddle, but was just annoyed enough to say, "I'm not so old. Who are you?"

"Don't mess with me or my woman, you son of a bitch!"

Jealousy wears a green face. "You must be Rick Black," I said.

"She told you about me, did she?" He stepped

nearer. "You stay away from her. You hear me? You and all the others!"

I stepped back and showed him my wedding ring. "Maria is a grown woman. She can decide who she wants to see. But it won't be me, because I already have all the woman I can handle."

But the ring seemed to enflame rather than soothe him. "You married bastards are the worst scum of all!" His voice was an explosion. He swung hard at my jaw.

I avoided most of the impact but his hard knuckles still gave me a jolt. He followed with a left hand that I caught on my right forearm. He was strong and fast, but he was a carpenter, not a boxer. I got away from him and held up both hands, palms out.

"You're after the wrong man, Black! Stop it!"

But he didn't stop. He came storming after me, full of rage and frustration. I backed onto Dodie's lawn, catching most of his blows on my arms. Then, when he kept coming, I suddenly stepped forward inside his swing. I got my arms around him and brought my knee up. He made an agonized sound and the strength went out of him. I let him fall. He lay doubled up on the ground clutching his crotch and groaning that groan emitted by every man who's ever taken a hard one in the balls.

I was breathing hard and feeling both glad that he was down and I was standing, and bad that it had come to this.

After a minute I knelt beside him and said, "Maria Donawa is a pretty girl, but she means nothing to me and I mean nothing to her. She came to see me on business. I advise you to remember that she doesn't belong to you or anybody else. You forget that and the next time you tangle with some guy, he may kill you or you may kill him. Either way it'll be for nothing. How are you feeling?"

He just groaned. There were tears of pain on his face. I wondered if I'd hurt him badly and wished I'd tried some other way of stopping him. Too late now.

I stood and glanced at the house. Dodie hadn't noticed a thing. I walked to the truck and drove home.

— 16 —

Maria phoned an hour later and I told her what I wanted her to do.

"All right," she said, "but I'm going to have a hard time explaining it."

"Don't explain. Let it be a mystery."

"It's already a mystery to me. Why do you want it?"

"I'll tell you later, when I give you my report."

"All right. I'll bring it by in the morning. Have you found out anything yet?"

"Not enough to mean anything. I'll see you in the morning."

"What was that all about?" asked Zee, who was setting the table for supper.

I told her.

"You're serious about this job you took," she said. Then she came close and touched the red mark on my jaw. "And what's this?"

"I was playing with the big boys. It's nothing."

"It doesn't look like nothing to me. You're not a kid anymore, Jefferson. Who was it?"

I told her.

She didn't like what she heard, and told me so.

"I didn't start it," I said, "and he kept coming."

"You should have run or yelled for help."

"Maybe you're right. I don't think he got hurt too badly."

"You didn't need to hurt him at all!" She turned away, then, just as fast, turned back. "And he could have hurt you!"

"Next time I'll run and yell."

"No, you won't."

"Yes, I will. I promise."

"You've said that before. I don't want any next times."

"Okay, no more next times. See how cooperative I can be?" I reached out and put my arms around her. She pushed against them, but not too hard.

Then she sighed and put her arms up around my neck. "I worry about you, Jefferson. I really do."

I kissed her and she kissed me back.

"Ma, how soon's supper?" asked Diana the huntress, looking for food as usual.

Her mother and I untangled. "It's almost ready," said Zee. "Go tell your brother to wash his hands and come to the table."

"Quality family time," I said. "There's nothing like it. You, me, and the kids, all together at the supper table. And the cats, of course."

"Get the casserole out of the oven," said Zee. "Maybe food will have charms to soothe your savage breast."

"Could be. I read somewhere that food, music, and sex can affect your brain in the same way."

Zee tossed her head. "Of course for that to happen you have to have a brain."

Wisely, I did not respond but put the casserole on the table and turned to meet Joshua and Diana as they came in, followed by Oliver Underfoot and Velcro.

"Pa."

"What, Josh?"

"Can we have a dog?"

It was not the first time the question had been asked in our house, nor was my answer new.

"No. No dogs. We have cats."

"If we had a little dog, she could play with the cats."

"No. Especially no little dog! When I'm king of the world I'm banning all small dogs. I thought I'd told you that."

"Ah, Pa. All our friends have dogs!"

"Then you can go play with their dogs. See, Oliver Underfoot and Velcro agree with me."

We all looked at the cats, who unmistakably did side with me on the dog issue.

"I don't think they agree with you," said Diana. "I think they agree with Joshua and me." She grinned a wicked little grin just like her mother's and put her arms around my leg. "Please, Pa!"

I held firm. "No. No dogs, and that's final. Now, wash up and come to dinner."

It was a pretty silent meal but it all got eaten.

The next morning, Maria Donawa stopped on her way to work and gave me a plastic bag containing the mug that her mother had identified as the one John Reilley traditionally used for coffee.

"Here," she said. "By the time I get home tonight Mom will miss it."

"Tell her you don't know where it is."

"I don't like lying to her."

"You won't be lying because you won't know where it is or what happened to it."

"All right. I just hope this is important."

"I'll let you know. Thanks for bringing it by."

She looked unhappy but went on to work.

Zee and the kids were also headed out, to the hospital and to school respectively. Only unemployed me had no obligation to be anywhere except where I wanted to be. I wanted to be in Aquinnah, so that's where I went, after making a phone call to make sure that Joe Begay would be home.

Aquinnah was known for hundreds of years as Gay Head but now once again officially possessed the name given to the area by the Wampanoags, who were living there long before the Europeans arrived. It is the Vineyard's westernmost township, and is the site of the wonderful colored clay cliffs that had given the place its English name. It is a lovely little town, geographically, and is famous for the striped bass that many a surf caster has caught there.

It is, alas, also known for its convoluted town politics, second only to those of Oak Bluffs as a subject of laughter for the citizens of the rest of the island, and for ripping off the tourists who come by the carload and busload to enjoy its beaches and the lovely cliffs.

There are NO PARKING signs along every road, so fishermen can no longer haunt the beaches as of yore; the town parking lot charges hapless drivers an arm and a leg; and, worst of all, the only toilets in town cost fifty cents a flush. Pay toilets are an abomination in the eyes of man and God at all times, but particularly when their users are trapped, tight-bladdered, elderly tourists unloaded from buses. I happily bad-mouth Aquinnah whenever given the chance and only go there to visit friends who have yards where I can park for free.

One of these was Joe Begay, who was married to

Toni, Zee's friend and one of the town's Vanderbeck women. Joe himself was raised in Oraibi, on the Hopi reservation, but was now settled on the Vineyard. Most of the time, anyway. Now and then he went off to Washington or elsewhere to do something for the gray-and-black-ops organization from which he was supposedly retired.

I never asked him about his work and he never talked much about it, but I'd known him since he'd been my sergeant long ago in Vietnam, and in the years since then had come to trust him to have useful contacts. Because he claimed I'd saved his life, he sometimes did me favors. Since I believed that he'd been the one who had saved my life, I tried not to take advantage of our friendship. But this was a time when I would if I could.

Joe and Toni lived just north of the cliffs. A sandy path led from their place to the beach, from which you could look out toward Devil's Bridge, where, over a century before, the *City of Columbus* had come to grief and spewed frozen bodies all along the Vineyard's western shores.

I parked in front of the house and he opened the door as I crossed the porch.

"Come in and get warm. I don't think I'm ever going to get used to this New England cold weather. Out where I come from the air is dry and you can walk around when it's below zero. Here I seize up when it gets below thirty."

"It ain't the heat, it's the humidity, like they say."

Joe Begay was tall and big in the chest but was a lot smaller in the hips. There was a scar on his forehead from a shrapnel wound that had blinded him for a while and later made his eyes so sensitive to light that he now almost always wore dark glasses during the day. Shrapnel from that same blast had left a lot of interesting scars on my legs. For both of us it had been the end of active duty in that war and the beginning of long stays in hospitals.

Now he handed me a cup of coffee and waved at a chair.

I gave him the plastic bag I'd brought and sat down. He peeked inside the bag.

"It's a coffee cup," I said. "I think it's got finger-prints on it, probably at least two sets. The woman is Dodie Donawa, who lives here on the island. The man calls himself John Reilley. I'd like to know if his prints belong to any other name, and if they do I'd like to know as much about him as I can. It's possible that he killed a man forty years ago, maybe near New Orleans or some other place down South."

Begay closed the bag and picked up his own cup. "What's this Reilley guy to you? You on a job of some kind, or just sticking your nose where it may not belong?"

"I'm doing a favor for a friend who wants to know if Reilley is the sweet guy her mother thinks he is. I told her I'd try to check him out."

"The daughter seems right to be suspicious, if you think he killed somebody. What makes you think he did?"

"He told me."

"Did he, now? Most people don't admit to that sort of thing." A small smile played across Begay's broad face.

"I got the impression he was glad to get it off his chest," I said. I told him about Reilley's under-ground house.

Begay raised a brow. "Do you believe him?"

I shrugged. "I'd like to check him out."

"Well," said Begay, "you've gotten me interested enough to make the effort. I'll have to send this cup to somebody, and it'll be a couple of days before I can get back to you."

"Fine." I sat back. "How are Toni and the tots?"

"The kids are in school, and Toni's up on the cliffs getting the shop ready for summer. Nowadays tourists start coming by in May. The season's getting longer every year."

"More money for all you original Americans."

Toni Begay's shop on the top of the cliffs, like others there and elsewhere on the island, carries souvenirs of Martha's Vineyard that are made in China. Unlike most of the other Aquinnah shops, hers also carries crafts that really were made by Indians, some of them actual Wampanoags. After the busloads of elderly tourists first spend their fifty-cent pieces at the town toilets down the hill, they spend more at the shops up the hill. Toni gets her share.

"And how are things down at the east end of Paradise?" asked Begay. "Is Mr. Fox still terrifying the locals?"

"Don't be so superior," I said. "Just because Fox isn't after your place doesn't mean he won't be here next."

"Not a chance," said Begay. "The white eyes already stole almost all the land belonging to us officially recognized original Americans. Now the government is on our side. Washington is so embarrassed about the Indian wars that now it'll defend our sacred soil against all comers, including Fox, and Fox is smart enough to know it."

I knew he was right. "How come all the land the local Wampanoags own or want is sacred?" I asked, just to be ornery.

He smiled. "That's easy. All of it is worth a lot of money, and my wife's people are Native Americans, and to an American nothing is more sacred than money."

"You win the box of Mars bars," I said. "I have no more questions."

— 17 —

In Chilmark I pulled off Middle Road into the driveway that led to the house that John Reilley was working on, parked out of sight, and walked up to a place where I could see who was there. By and by I spotted Rick Black move in and out of view. I was glad that he seemed to have recovered from the blow he'd taken. A bit later John Reilley came out of a doorway, picked up a circular saw, and returned inside. I went back to my car and, after making sure that no one was following me, drove to the state forest, where I parked in the lot fronting the official but currently empty Frisbee golf range.

I've never played Frisbee golf, but I was glad there was a course for those who do. I got my pocket flashlight, zipped my down vest, and walked out on the range. Then, after again checking to make sure no one was observing me, I cut into the woods.

The trees were still bare of leaves, so I could see farther than would be the case during the summer. Even so, there wasn't a lot to see. I picked my way through the forest, making a big circle and stopping now and then to glance back over my trail. No tailing Indians or Daniel Boones were in evidence, so I went on until I came to the cellar hole that contained the door to John Reilley's house. I gave a final

360-degree examination of the empty forest, saw no one, and dropped down into the depression.

Years before I had found a set of lock picks on a yard sale table, and had bought them for a dollar from the widow who was selling her late husband's possessions and who, I was sure, had no idea what they were. I'd wondered at the time what he had done for a living, but I hadn't asked. Now the picks were in my pocket, but, as it turned out, I didn't need them.

John, I reasoned, would not have a metal lock on his door because it would too easily be seen. Rather, the door would be fastened shut in some simple but unobtrusive way. I studied the apparent jumble of boards that made up the door, then began to run my hands behind them.

After a short time, voilà! I found a knob of wood and pushed it and turned it until, silently, the door opened. I followed my flashlight inside and shut the door behind me, then flipped on the electrical switch I'd spotted on my earlier visit. The house filled with light.

The room was just as I'd left it. I studied its walls but saw no photographs. I crossed to a bookcase and examined the books it contained. No ex libris names were to be found. A couple of the books were in Spanish, though, indicating that John read at least one more language than I did.

I went through a low doorway into the kitchen, where I opened every cabinet door and drawer. No diamonds were hidden in the ice cubes, none of the cookbooks had a name scribbled inside the binding. A closet held a box of paper bags from the A&P, cleaning supplies and tools, and odds and ends of household stuff you just might need some day. Exactly the contents of my kitchen closet and maybe everybody's kitchen closet.

I went down a narrow hallway and found a ladder that led upward. I went up the ladder, passing cables holding metal weights as I went. At the top there was a hinged metal hatch, and I realized that the weights and cables formed some sort of counterbalance to the weight of the hatch. The latch seemed to be the kind that could be unfastened from both inside and out. I loosened it and pushed the hatch up. It rose easily. I contented myself with opening it only a few inches so I could look out. I seemed to be on the far side of the tree beyond a patch of greenbrier where Reilley secreted his moped when he was at home. I took some bearings and lowered the hatch and fastened it. A rear door is often handy.

I went back to the kitchen and went into what turned out to be Reilley's bedroom. It was small but comfortable, with a single bed, a chair and desk, a bureau with a mirror, more bookcases, and a long curtain across the far end that covered a closet. An adjoining alcove contained a chemical toilet, a washbasin, and a small shower stall that looked like it had originally been made for a boat. I doubted if Reilley used the shower much, since he had to pack in all of his water, and recalled his comment that he showered in the houses he helped build.

I went through all of the drawers in the bureau and the desk and found nothing that might tell me more about John Reilley: no letters, no diary, no memoirs, no ladies' underwear. There was a bankbook from an off-island bank. John Reilley had a couple of thousand dollars there. The address on the book was John's PO box number in Vineyard Haven.

I lifted the mattress and looked under the bed. No goblins, no trolls, no nothing.

I leafed through the books. No names, no perfumed notes between the pages, no bookmarks from bookstores in New Orleans.

John Reilley had left no paper trail. A careful guy. I liked his taste in books, though. Good stuff. No junk except maybe for some paperback Western novels written by guys with manly sounding names. I didn't have time to read any of them, so they might have been good, too.

I looked in every closet and cubbyhole and found nothing of interest.

I left the house as I'd found it, turned off the lights, peeked out the peephole to make sure nobody was outside, locked the door behind me, and walked around to the far side of the tree where John kept his moped.

It took me a while to spot the location of the rear exit's hatch. It was a rotten-looking stump. I thought about the location of the latch inside, and found the outside latch under a lichen-covered rock that looked as if it hadn't been moved in years. When I worked the latch, the stump tipped back, revealing the hole beneath. I pushed it shut and replaced the rock, then went out of the woods a different way than I'd come in and walked back along the empty bike path to my truck.

As I drove home I thought about the shooting and what had happened since. The shots had been long ones for a pistol, and the shooter hadn't come close to hitting Donald Fox.

So he wasn't much of a marksman.

Or maybe he was. He'd put two bullets close together right over Paul Fox's heart.

When I got to the house I called Dom Agganis.

"Any new news?" I asked.

"None of your business," said Dom. "Okay, I'll tell you this much: some guy going into the Black Dog heard the shots and thinks he saw a man run out of sight toward that place that makes the wooden boats."

"Gannon and Benjamin."

"Whatever. Anyway, the hungry guy says the other guy went off in that direction. He didn't see a gun."

"Any description?"

"The useless kind. Winter clothes, medium height, medium build, no distinguishing characteristics."

I'd learned one thing: Agganis wasn't a wooden boat man. If he had been, he'd have known that Gannon and Benjamin was a yard that does fine work building and repairing only wooden boats.

"Anybody at the boatyard see anything?" I asked.

"No," said Agganis. "My own guess is that the guy was probably walking by then and didn't attract any attention. I figure he had a car out by the road somewhere."

"That's why I called," I said. "You might check around and see if anybody saw one of those green Range Rovers parked someplace nearby. Maybe somebody even saw the guy get into it and drive away."

I could imagine Dom's eyes becoming hooded. "Why do you say that? You know something?"

"It's just that I think it's possible that the shooter was tied to Saberfox."

"How?"

"I don't know."

"You're just guessing, then."

"It's a little more than a guess." I told him about Reston and Wall. "Donald Fox seemed pretty surprised and angry when I told him about them following me," I said. "Something's going on in the company that the big boss says he doesn't know about."

Dom was silent for a minute, then said, "Anything else?"

"One more question. Did you find Kirkland's laptop computer in his car or in his house?"

Dom's ears seemed to go up. "What laptop computer?"

"Kirkland had a laptop computer when he came to our house. He carried it instead of a briefcase. If you found it, you might check it out in case Kirkland recorded something that could shed some light on this case. Well?"

"Well, what?"

"Well, did you find his computer?"

"No. Maybe he kept it at the company office when he wasn't on the road."

"Maybe. Will you let me know?"

"Maybe. I'll tell you one thing that might interest you. I took a photo of Kirkland down to the Fireside and showed it to Bonzo. He ID'ed the guy he saw in the Range Rover as Kirkland."

"Another mystery solved."

"Every little bit helps. Right now I think I'll run down to Saberfox's office and ask some questions. Maybe I'll run into Paul Fox and he'll tell me what I want to know. His big brother won't say a word with-

out his lawyer standing beside him, and that recep-
tionist is just as bad."

"Can I come along?"

"No." He hung up.

Rejected once again. Maybe it was my breath.
But I didn't mind because I already had something
to do.

18

Rick Black wasn't listed in the phone book, and directory assistance informed me that his number was unlisted. Secretive Rick.

But I had a source of information. I called Dodie Donawa and learned not only Rick's telephone number but also that he lived on Oak Lane in West Tisbury. Dodie didn't know just where on Oak Lane, but that was no problem. I called the West Tisbury police station, identified myself as a lost driver for FedEx with a package to deliver to Richard Black, who lived somewhere on Oak Lane. The helpful police officer told me which house was Rick's.

Oak Lane is a long street that leads southeast off Old County Road. Some of its houses are the summer kind, which are empty during the rest of the year. Rick Black's place was a small, fairly new house on the left. I drove by slowly and took a good look at it for signs of activity. I saw none, then had a bit of good luck in that the next place down the road was one of those empty summerhouses.

I parked in the driveway of the summerhouse, put on a pair of tight rubber gloves, palmed my lock picks, and walked back to Black's house. I'm not the world's champion lock picker, but then Rick Black's doors didn't have world champion locks on them, so after knocking and having no one answer, I was inside in short order.

I went through the house room by room and decided, from the number of travel and sailing magazines I found, that Rick apparently fantasized about visiting far-off countries and owning a large yacht.

For a bachelor he kept a fairly neat house, but his pantry, refrigerator, and rubbish containers revealed him as a guy who lived mostly out of cans and cartons and who drank light beer. No wonder he'd lost that fight with me.

I found his shotgun in a closet and his fishing and shellfishing gear in the basement, but I didn't find any sign of a handgun or an interest in one. There were no gun magazines, leather, boxes of bullets, or other suggestions that Rick was a pistoleer in fact or in fancy.

He had a good collection of well-maintained wood tools and there was a photo of Maria Donawa on his mantel. She was smiling at the camera. The picture had been taken during happier times for Rick.

A car went by on the road, and as soon as it was gone I went out the way I'd come in, got back to the truck, and drove away. I didn't want to risk having more than one passing driver remember that my Land Cruiser had been parked in Rick's neighbor's driveway.

It had been several days since Paul Fox had been shot outside the E and E Deli and I had gotten involved with the inner circle of Saberfox. During those days Albert Kirkland had been killed, I'd been tailed by Wall and Reston, I'd found John Reilley's underground lair, and I'd been attacked by Rick Black.

It had been a busy few days. In fact, it had been a busy morning. But now it was noon and I was hungry, so I drove to Edgartown and had lunch at the Newes From America, which offers good pub food and excellent beer. I had the twenty-ounce glass of Red Tail ale while I ate my fried calamari and ran things through my mind. By the time my glass and plate were empty I had an afternoon plan and some thoughts that were less fuzzy than before.

I headed for Saberfox headquarters in Oak Bluffs.

Dana Hvide still guarded the gateway. I told her I wanted to talk with Donald Fox and she told me that he wasn't in the office. I asked her where I could find him and she said she didn't know. I didn't believe her, but asked her to tell him, the next time she saw or heard from him, that I wanted to see him. She said she would do that. I asked her where I could find Paul Fox and she said she didn't know. I didn't believe her some more. I asked her if Saberfox reps left their computers in the office every night, and she said no. I smiled and thanked her and left.

The first person I saw when I went into the ER at the hospital was my wife, who had her back to me as she talked to a boy who looked so young that I knew he must be a doctor. Zee has very fine lines, and I admired them as I approached and gave her a surprise smooch on the neck. She turned and smiled.

"What are you doing here? Are you an emergency?"

"You don't look startled. Do you get kisses on the neck regularly?"

"All the time. Other places, too. What brings you to this temple of healing if you don't need our expert care? Oh, by the way, this is Dr. Fred DaMoura. Fred, this is my husband, Hot Lips."

Fred and I shook hands. "Nice to know you, Hot Lips," he said.

"You, too, Fred." I watched him move away, then put my hands on Zee's shoulders. "I'm actually looking for another woman. Maybe you can help me. I'll come back to you when I'm through with her."

"Lucky me. Who is this poor woman who has you in her future?"

"Maria Donawa. I know she works here somewhere, but I don't know where."

I got directions to Maria's desk, walked through a couple of halls until I found it, and said hello.

"Why, hello yourself, J.W. What brings you here?"

"I'm looking for Paul Fox. I figured you might know where he is. How's he feeling these days?"

She sat back. "He's still got pretty sore ribs, but he's feeling better. Donald wants him to go back to Savannah, but he won't do it."

"He probably thinks he has a good reason to stay here."

She smiled a bit primly. "He may be right. I'm not sure where he is right now. He may be out with Donald somewhere, but sometimes, if his ribs are hurting, he takes a little rest in the afternoon before he goes back to work. So he may be in his suite. Donald won't let him work if he's feeling tired. They're very close." She scribbled on a piece of paper and handed it to me. "Paul's learning the business end of things now, but Donald wants him to take all the time he needs to get better."

"Maybe Paul wants to get married and settle down and he thinks he needs a steady job."

"Maybe he does." Then her smile changed to a frown. "But I don't like the idea of him working for Saberfox."

"The real estate and development business probably isn't any worse than any other business, and there's certainly plenty of money in it."

"It's a lot worse the way Saberfox does it!"

"If Paul takes over, he can change company policy."

She nodded. "That would be good, but nothing will change as long as Donald and Brad Hillborough are running things."

"I didn't know Hillborough ran things."

She sighed. "I guess he really doesn't, but his loyalty is to Donald, not to Paul. He doesn't want any changes Donald doesn't want. It's hard for anyone to turn a company around when the old guard is against change."

That was probably true. I didn't mention the possibility that Saberfox might change Paul more than Paul might change Saberfox. Instead, I thanked her for her help, returned to the ER, gave Zee another kiss, and left the hospital.

Paul Fox's apartment was on the first floor of the Martin's Vineyard Hotel, downstairs from the Saberfox offices, where, not long before, Dana Hvide had assured me that she had no idea where Paul was.

Maybe she really didn't. Maybe he was off with his brother somewhere. But I parked and knocked on his door anyway and was pleasantly surprised when he opened it.

"Mr. Jackson, come in."

His suite had been decorated by some New England minimalist with a liking for white walls and furniture. All that white made the place a bit too bright but it was otherwise comfortable enough. Paul Fox sat me in a soft white chair beside a white coffee table and eased himself carefully down in its twin.

"I'm still a little tender," he said apologetically, "but it's getting better every day."

"I've never known anybody who enjoyed being shot," I said. "I'd like to talk with you about Saberfox. Your brother doesn't let much out about the business, but I'm hoping I can learn a bit from you."

He became wary. "What do you want to know? Why?"

I touched first one finger then the next, then the next. "You were shot, Albert Kirkland was murdered, two guys named Wall and Reston have been following me. The common denominator is Saberfox. I need to know more about the company than I do now."

"Wall and Reston have been following you? Are you sure?"

"Your brother thinks it's them. He says he knows nothing about it."

"Nor do I." He ran a hand across his face, the way some people do when they're trying to think their way out of confusion, and stared at me silently. Then he got up and crossed the room to a desk and came back. He handed me a brochure. "This tells you all about the company."

"I'll read it," I said. "But what I want to know isn't written on a piece of paper. I need to know about the people inside, including Reston and Wall. What they think, what they feel, where their loyalties lie, what they argue about."

He shook his head uncomfortably. "If Donald won't talk about that, I won't either."

I pulled out his IOU. "I may have saved your life when I hauled you out of the street, Paul. This will make us even. I don't want business secrets, I want to know what you know about the psychodynamics of the top level of the company: who hates who, who loves who, who has an ax to grind. I'm looking for a killer and I need help."

"There aren't any killers working for Saberfox," he said. Then his hand strayed to his chest and he made his decision. "All right, I do owe you something, but I don't know what to tell you. I don't know exactly what you want to know."

I wasn't sure myself. "Let's start at the beginning," I said. "Tell me how Donald got going in this business. It's a big operation. How did it start?"

He sat back in his soft white chair and stared with unfocused eyes at a spot just over my head.

I waited, wondering if he was going to tell me the truth or some true-sounding, self-serving lie.

When he was satisfied with his thoughts, he brought his gaze back to my eyes.

"It was fencing that made it possible," he said. "I guess we can start there."

19

"Donald was always a good athlete, but he was a prodigious talent as a fencer, particularly in saber. He got a scholarship to New York University and won the NCAA saber championship during his junior and senior years. Then, as you probably know, he became the only American to win a gold medal in Olympic fencing. He was twenty-three."

"Pretty impressive," I said.

Paul Fox nodded. "Yes. He had that monomaniacal focus that it takes to be a champion. He had no life other than studying and fencing, and looking after me."

I raised a brow.

Seeing it, he went on. "Our parents were dead, killed in one of those car wrecks you hear about too often: a drunk crossed into their lane and hit them head-on. The drunk lived, of course, but they died. I was ten years old and Donald was in college. Insurance kept us going until he was through school, and after that he paid my way. I was never half the athlete he was and my grades weren't good enough for a big scholarship, but he parlayed his gold medals into business opportunities, and the same intensity that made him a champion fencer made him the successful businessman he's become. He took care of me through school, and now I'm working for him."

"He doesn't have the reputation of being generous."
Fox frowned. "As a fencer he was cold as ice and never popular in spite of his success. He didn't care. Winning was everything. He's never had time for social graces. He never married and he doesn't have friends. He doesn't let down his guard to anyone but me. I'm his whole family." He paused. "Except, maybe, for Brad Hillborough."

"Hillborough?"

"Yes. Brad lives for my brother, and he'd die for him. You saw that cane of his. He's never once complained about what it cost him to save Donald's life."

"How'd they meet?"

"Brad was on the NYU fencing team with Donald, although he was never of championship caliber. But unlike others, he didn't resent Donald's success. Instead, he became the closest thing Donald had to a friend. He majored in physical therapy and became Donald's personal trainer while they were still in college. He took responsibility for my brother's diet and exercise routine, massaged him, cared for his bruises and sprains, and did it all gladly. He kept it up through the Olympics, and when Donald went into business afterward, Brad went with him. He's still Donald's trainer."

I thought Hillborough's devotion sounded like that of a dog, but I only said, "Sancho Panza. Watson. The faithful, trusted friend."

"Yes. And Donald has needed such a friend, because he has no others and trusts no one else except me."

"How do you and Hillborough get along?"

"He tolerates me. I don't think he trusts me to be as competent as my brother and he's probably right to doubt, because I'm different from Donald. I lack his killer instinct. Brad doesn't approve of the people I've brought into the firm, either." He looked at me from beneath lowered lids. "You mentioned two of them: Peter Wall and Chris Reston. You say they've been following you. Do you know why?"

"Why don't you ask them? If you find out let me know. Why did you bring them into Saberfox?"

"Peter and Chris were my best friends in college. They're research-oriented and educated in business, just the sort of people Saberfox needs to ferret out questionable land titles."

"A sorry kind of work," I said.

"You may be right, but it's legal and it's profitable. It's one of the things that Saberfox does, and Peter and Chris are good at digging through old records. Brad is suspicious of them anyway, probably because he thinks their loyalty is to me rather than to Donald."

"Are there people he trusts?"

"A couple, maybe. There was one more until last week: Al Kirkland. He and Al weren't close, but he trusted Al."

"It sounds to me as though there are two factions in the inner circle: you and your friends, and your brother, Brad Hillborough, and their friends."

"I don't think my brother would consider any of his employees friends, with the possible exception of Brad, and I'm not even sure if Brad is an exception."

"Brad apparently feels some sort of special tie to your brother."

"Yes." Fox frowned and shrugged.

"Does Hillborough have a family?"

"No. Saberfox is his family. My brother is the closest thing he has to kin."

"Your brother is a handsome, wealthy man," I said. "I'd think that there'd be women in his life."

"I know what you're thinking," said Paul, showing me a crooked smile, "but I assure you that my brother is not a homosexual. There have been many women in his life, but none for very long. He uses them and they use him and they go their own ways. Maybe when Donald has earned all of the money he thinks he needs, he'll marry and start a dynasty to inherit his empire."

I thought he'd have no problem finding a wife, since I was at least a semi-believer in the old saw that men cannot resist beauty and women cannot resist money.

"And where will that leave you?" I asked.

"I have a trust fund. Donald set it up for me. I don't need to work."

"Then why do you?"

"Because I don't enjoy being a slug. Most people don't."

I thought he was right. Most of the moneyed people I know work hard at something: sport, volunteerism, or figuring out how to make more money or give away what they have. It had been one of my most surprising self-discoveries when I learned that I wasn't happy being lazy. I'd always thought I was a natural sloth.

"What do you know about Albert Kirkland?"

"I know that Brad Hillborough knew him and brought him into the firm. My impression was that Brad wanted at least one person he could trust completely. Kirkland was good at his work, of course. Brad is incredibly defensive about Saberfox and would never hire an incompetent."

"Was Kirkland more loyal to Brad or to Saberfox?"

Paul's brow furled. "I never thought of the question. I don't know the answer."

"What was his background? His education? Where did he and Brad Hillborough meet?"

"I don't know about his education, but he and Brad met at the Olympic trials when Al was trying out for the pentathlon. Why do you need to know?"

"Is there a file on Kirkland? Something the company would have kept on each of its employees?"

"If there is it's in Savannah, and I've never seen it. Why are you so interested in Al Kirkland? He's the victim, not the killer."

"There are always two stories in killings," I said. "The killer's and the victim's. They start out apart and they come together. If I can learn Kirkland's story, maybe I can figure out how he got himself killed. That's why I need to know about you. So I can figure out who wants you dead."

He shook his head. "Nobody wants me dead. I don't have any enemies at all. Those shots were meant for my brother. I don't like to admit it, but a lot of people hate him enough to kill him. That's why I was wearing armor that day. I wanted to see if it was uncomfortable or inconvenient before I asked him to wear it."

"He was very happy that you were wearing that vest."

He smiled. "Me, too. I'd actually been wearing it for several days but nobody knew it. Now Donald is considering wearing one, too, so it was worth taking those bullets."

"Has anyone else tried to shoot him?"

"No, but people are always attacking Donald. In

court, in the papers. A few people have even tried to assault him. The worst was that woman in the car who tried to run him down."

"But Brad Hillborough saved him."

"Yes, at considerable cost to himself. But Brad couldn't stop them all. One man got past Brad and hit Donald. He didn't hurt him. What happened then was worse. Donald pretended he'd been challenged to a duel. The man had been a fencer and Donald shamed him into meeting him with sabers."

"That would be akin to murder. The man must have been a fool."

"Worse yet, he fancied himself a Southern gentleman who was obliged to save face. His face was about all he saved, as it turned out."

"Your brother was a world champion. He must have chopped him to pieces."

"Oh, no. They didn't use cavalry sabers, they used the fencing kind. You know, with the thin blades. But did you ever take a slash across the back by a heavy-handed saber fencer? It's worse than a blacksnake whip.

"My brother didn't kill him, he slashed him to his knees until he wept with pain and couldn't even stand. The fellow was welts and cuts from his waist to his neck. Donald was careful not to hit his face, and made sure there was a doctor on hand. The man still has the scars, and he's more of a mouse now than a lion."

"Weren't charges brought against your brother?"

"No. It had been agreed that if anyone asked it had been a fencing lesson. Word got out, but no one ever officially asked about what had happened."

"The doctor didn't speak up?"

"He, too, was a Southern gentleman and it had been an affair of honor."

Honor. A word that has caused a lot more bad than good.

"What had your brother done to make the man so angry?"

Paul Fox raised his eyes. "Saberfox had taken possession of his mother's house. It was just business as far as Donald was concerned."

"Did Donald enjoy the duel?"

"He never said. He did tell me that he wanted people to know that it was unwise to attack him or Saberfox."

"But now you think that someone's taken a shot at him," I said. "That may be a criminal act, but it sounds safer than meeting under the oak at dawn."

"My brother may not be the nicest guy in town but he doesn't deserve to be murdered! Everything Saberfox does is legal. Donald was poor when he was young and now he plans to be rich, and to make me rich, too, whether or not people are happy about the way he does it."

I only had one more question: "You and your brother are living under the same roof here. Did you live together in Savannah, too?"

"No. I had my own place. I wasn't involved in the business down there, but I decided I wanted to work for Saberfox about the time we came north. When Donald learned that, he found me this place. At first it was so he could keep an eye on me, but now we can talk business in the evenings. Since the shooting, he's decided to teach me everything he can, so if he ever leaves Saberfox, or if anything happens to him, I can take over."

"Even though you lack his killer instinct?"

"I think he expects me to develop one, although to tell you the truth, I'm not sure I want to. I think Saberfox can thrive without robbing people of their homes."

"You'll have to have a thick skin to run a business with a reputation like Saberfox has."

"Maybe I can change the way the company works."

"Or maybe the company and your brother will change the way you work."

"Maybe."

I left him and went out. As I drove along Old County Road I noticed a green Range Rover following me. It irked me so badly that I decided to do something about it.

20

I drove slowly home so the Range Rover could follow me without difficulty. When I turned into our long, sandy driveway, I glanced in the rearview mirror and saw it go by the driveway entrance with the driver's face turned my way. I'd had half a hope that he'd follow me to my house, but apparently he was not ready to do that.

I went into the house and unlocked the case where we kept our guns. Inside were my father's shotguns and deer rifle, Zee's target pistols, and the old .38 police revolver I'd carried when on the Boston PD long ago. I loaded the .38 and put it under my belt, drove back to the highway, and turned toward Vineyard Haven. In the rearview mirror I saw the Range Rover pull out of a side road and fall in behind me.

Good.

There were abandoned housing developments in several places on posh Martha's Vineyard, victims of economic declines between booms. But we were booming again now, and where many rutted roads once led to unfinished foundations, there were now paved lanes lined with huge new houses.

But not every failure had yet become a success, and there were still dirt roads that wound through trees and oak brush leading nowhere. One of them led off the Edgartown–Vineyard Haven highway. I turned onto the road and followed its windings to its bitter end, where it looped back on itself around a pile of large boulders once intended to grace the entrances to houses that were never built, and big enough to hide the old Land Cruiser from the sight of following vehicles.

I parked on the far side of the boulders, got out, and skulked back to a spot behind an evergreen. I'd barely gotten there when the Range Rover came bouncing into view. It passed me as it started around the loop and came to a sudden stop behind my truck. When it did that I walked up to the driver's door and tapped on the glass.

The driver stared at me, then looked around at the empty forest. The lack of houses and people seemed to encourage him. He said something to the man in the passenger seat and pushed open his door. I stepped back as he came out. His partner came around the front of the Range Rover. Both of them were tall and wide and pulling on leather gloves.

"You two will ruin your health breathing my exhaust all of the time," I said. "Besides, I feel like I'm sailing with an anchor dragging over the stern. It's time we had a talk. What do you two want, anyway?"

"You've made a mistake," said the first man, with a grim smile. "There are two of us and you're out here all alone."

"What do you want?"

"Some straight answers, to start with." The two of them seemed to lean toward me. I took some comfort in the fact that they both wore buttoned overcoats with no bulges in the pockets.

"Which one are you?" I asked. "Wall or Reston?"

They exchanged quick glances. "I'm Wall," said the first man. "You know our names, do you? How'd you work that out? Not that it makes any difference. We know who you are, that's what's important. You tried to kill Paul Fox because of that girl!"

They were aware of their size. They stepped forward. I stepped back and said, "I thought the theory was that Donald was the target and the shooter was just bad at his work. A lot of people would be glad to shoot Donald."

"Don't give us that crap. I don't give a damn about Donald, but you weren't shooting at him, you were shooting at Paul, and if the police don't think they have enough evidence now to arrest you, they'll have it when we're through with you. You're going to be sorry you ever tried such a thing, and you're going to talk. First to us, then to them. Your murdering days are over."

"You have more confidence in the law than I do," I said. "On Martha's Vineyard nobody does time. Just look at the court reports in the paper if you don't believe me, or ask a cop. The people they arrest are back on the streets quicker than they can put them in jail."

"Then you can spend your time in the hospital instead of prison," said Reston, and they both came toward me.

I faded back and unzipped my coat. Then I stopped. "Slow down, boys," I said, and displayed the butt of the pistol in my belt. "You're wrong about me being alone. I have Smith and Wesson and six of their little copper-coated friends with me."

They stopped, hot-eyed and seeming to teeter on their toes.

"Is that the gun you used to shoot Paul, you son of a bitch?" asked Reston. "I should have known you're too much of a coward to go unarmed. What are you going to do, shoot us, too, like you shot him? You'll never get away with it."

"You're the bright boy who noticed that there's nobody out here but the three of us," I said, feeling angry now that the two men were hesitating. "Nobody saw us come in here and nobody will see me go out, so if I felt like shooting you this would be an excellent place to do it. Nobody would find your carcasses for days."

Reston seemed almost ready to jump me, gun or not, but Wall now eyed me carefully. He put out a hand to restrain Reston. "What do you mean, *if*?"

"What do you think I mean, you cluck? If I wanted to shoot you, you'd be shot already. Neither one of you would have made it out of the car." I shook my head. "The Chief said there were a couple of Saberfox vigilantes hot for scalps, but you're piss-poor at this kind of work, I can tell you that. Paul Fox has a lot higher opinion of you two than I do."

Reston looked surprised. "You've talked with Paul?"

"I've talked with Donald, too, and everybody else I can think of who might have anything to do with this case. And now I'm even talking with you two tough guys. Incidentally, Donald has put those flunkies of his, Burns and Jacobs, on your case. I think your tails are in a noose."

"Wait a minute," said Reston. "Who the hell are you, anyway?"

I felt snippy. "I'm the guy you've been following all over this island. Who the hell do you think I am?"

"Black. You're Richard Black."

I stared at him, then shook my head. "What gave you that wacky idea? If I'm Rick Black, you're the king of Siam and your pal here is Anna."

The empty forest rang with silence. Then Wall said, "If you're not Black, who the hell are you and why have you been driving around in his car?"

Then I remembered Maria telling me that Rick had just gotten himself a new truck.

"This isn't Rick Black's truck," I said, waving a hand at the Toyota. "It's mine. And I'm not him, I'm J. W. Jackson. You've been tailing the wrong man, you meatheads!"

They exchanged looks.

I went on. "I get it. Your plan was to catch Rick somewhere private so you could beat a confession out of him. Wonderful. Why didn't you just go to his house and do it there?"

Wall looked embarrassed. "Because we don't know where he lives. He's not in the phone book."

"You could have asked somebody."

Reston blushed. "We didn't want anybody to know we were after him. Besides, who would we ask?"

Such innocence was almost appealing. "You're a fine pair of tough-guy detectives. I think you'd better get out of this line of work before you actually do some damage. Let the police handle this; it's their job and they're a lot better at it than you two. How'd you get on my tail in the first place?"

Wall answered that one. "Paul Fox told us about seeing Black driving off in a huff one night when Paul was picking up that Donawa woman he's dating. He described Black's car. We figured that after Black shot Paul, he'd be back chasing the girl, so we took turns watching the house. When his truck—I mean your truck—showed up two days ago, we followed it."

"Well, your intelligence is a little out-of-date. Since Paul saw Rick, Rick traded in that old Toyota on a new pickup."

"We didn't know that. We thought you were him." Wall paused and looked at the ground. "I know it sounds stupid."

I had been just as stupid from time to time, no doubt.

"It does indeed," I said. "Do you two do any drinking at the Fireside in OB?"

They exchanged blank looks.

"What's the Fireside?" asked Wall.

"Never mind," I said. "I think you'd better go back to work in the Registry of Deeds, stealing property from the lame and the halt for the greater glory of Saberfox. Leave vengeance to God and justice to Caesar. Besides, for what it's worth, I've looked at Rick Black's gun collection and there isn't a pistol in sight. And I know from personal experience that when he's mad he uses his fists instead of weapons. So I don't think he's your shootist. You were going to beat up the wrong guy." It was a long speech, and it made me tired.

"Well, if Black didn't do it, who did?" demanded Reston.

"There are about fifteen thousand people on this island right now," I said, "and unless the shooter's sailed to America he's one of the other fourteen thousand nine hundred and ninety-nine. Go back to the office and get a good story ready on your way. You'll need it when Donald Fox catches up with you. He doesn't like to have his people doing things he doesn't know about." I zipped up my coat, turned, and walked to the old Land Cruiser.

"We work for Paul Fox, not his brother," said Reston's voice behind me.

"And Paul works for Donald," I said without glancing back. "You can follow me back to the highway. I don't want you to get lost."

I climbed into the truck and drove home. The Range Rover trailed me to the pavement, then went the other way.

Reston and Wall might have to consider the other 14,999 people on the Vineyard, but I didn't. I was working on a shorter list. Most people get killed by people they know. I didn't think Kirkland knew too many people on Martha's Vineyard, but apparently he knew at least one who drove a dark-colored Range Rover. That narrowed my list considerably.

I was also interested by the number of fencers who had come to my attention lately: Donald Fox, Paul Fox, Brad Hillborough, and, if the pattern continued, probably somebody I didn't know about yet. Only Donald Fox was a champion, of course, but you don't have to be a champion to know which end of a sword does the damage. Kirkland had been killed with a long knife, and a sword was only a longer knife than most.

I was anxious to learn what Joe Begay could tell me about John Reilley. Before hearing from Joe, though, I got some news that surprised me. It came in the form of a phone call from Zee the next morning, just after she got to the hospital.

"Did you hear?" she asked. "They've arrested Rick Black for attempted murder."

21

"Maria just told me," said Zee. "Apparently the police
got an anonymous tip that the pistol fired at Paul Fox
could be found in Rick's house. They went up there
last night and found it."

I felt a frown form on my face. "An anonymous
tip usually doesn't earn you a search warrant."

"I don't know if they had a warrant. Maria says
that they were waiting when Rick came home from
work, and he let them go into the house. They found
the pistol and took it away and got somebody to
test-fire it and compared the bullet with the one in
Paul Fox's bulletproof vest, and this morning they
arrested Rick. He's down in the county jail right
now. I guess he doesn't know any lawyers, so he
called Dodie Donawa for help, and she told Maria."

And Maria told Zee and now Zee was telling me.
The truth usually gets lost in a verbal trail that long.

"I think they've got the wrong man," I said. "If
the police think Rick did it, they may stop looking
for the guy who really shot Paul."

"What makes you think that? Rick has a temper
and he's a violent man. He picked a fight with you
just the day before yesterday!"

"Fistfights and assassinations aren't the same," I
said. "You're right about Rick's temper, but the cops

are wrong about him owning that pistol. I'm going downtown."

"Wait," she said. "What do you know about the pistol?"

"I'll tell you later," I said, "when we're not talking on a phone. See you tonight."

I hung up, got into my coat, and drove to the County of Dukes County jail. It was my second trip to the jail in a week. I usually didn't go there once in a year.

There were all kinds of police cruisers parked in back. One belonged to the State Police, one to the sheriff's department, one to the Edgartown police, and one to the West Tisbury police. The cops had Rick considerably outnumbered. I parked beside the fuzz mobiles and went inside, where I was greeted mostly with grunts of recognition and expressionless faces. There was one exception.

"Our nice day has ended," said Officer Olive Otero. "Mr. Jackson has arrived."

I ignored her. "I hear you've got Rick Black in jail," I said to the room at large.

"You heard right," said Dom Agganis.

"I hear it's because you found the pistol that supposedly fired the bullet that damaged Paul Fox."

"No comment."

Olive looked pleased at her boss's briskly stated remark.

Edgartown's chief of police was drinking coffee out of a Styrofoam cup. I nodded to him. "Can I talk with you and Dom in private?"

The Chief and Agganis exchanged glances.

"Sure," said the Chief. "Let's step outside." He and

his coffee led the way and Dom Agganis rode drag with me between them.

Outside, we turned our collars up against the cold.

"This is off the record," I said.

Their eyes were expressionless.

The Chief sipped his coffee. "You know us both, J.W. We'll play it straight with you. But we won't be giving any carte blanche until we hear what you have to say."

Agganis nodded.

"Fair enough." I told them what I'd heard from Zee, then asked, "Is that about what happened?"

"That's about right."

"Well, someone who shall be nameless for the time being was in that house earlier in the afternoon and there was no pistol there. Was it pretty easy for the West Tisbury cops to find? Right there in the closet with Rick's shotgun, maybe?"

Agganis sighed and looked annoyed. "Dare I guess that the nameless someone is very near the Chief here, even as we speak?"

"You can guess whatever you want to, Dom. But I'm mentioning no names for the moment."

Agganis rolled his eyes. "All right. What was this nameless someone doing in Rick Black's house?"

"Maybe he got lost in the woods. Maybe he thought it was made of gingerbread. The point is that he was there and had a good look around just a few hours before the cops were there, and there was no pistol in sight."

Our breaths were little clouds of condensed vapor in the morning air.

"Was the tipster a man or a woman?" I asked, breaking the short silence.

"A man, probably. Voice was muffled. Made the call on a public phone up in Vineyard Haven. We can check on whether Black was at work all afternoon. If he was and if you and your nameless someone aren't just pulling our chains, maybe somebody's setting him up." Agganis looked at me. "Why was your somebody in his house snooping around? What was he doing there?"

"He was looking for the pistol you guys found. Black is a natural for the short list of suspects: Maria Donawa left him for Paul Fox, he's jealous, and he's got a temper. If he had the pistol that did the shooting, that would just about put him away. My someone would like to have this over and done with. Hell, so would I. I'm tired of being in the middle of it." I told them about Black's encounter with me two days before.

"Whoever stashed the gun apparently thinks the same way you do about Black being a good suspect," said the Chief. He sipped more of his coffee. "If Rick goes to trial, will your nameless somebody be willing to testify?"

"My somebody wouldn't like it, but he'd testify to what he knows."

"Then Rick Black can charge him with unlawful entry or worse, if he feels like it," said the Chief.

"Maybe he won't feel like it, if the testimony gets him off the hook," I said.

"Maybe not. We're going to have to tell the DA what you just told us. He'll probably want to talk with your somebody before he decides whether or not to formally charge Rick."

"I'll convey that message to my somebody."

"You make me tired sometimes," said Agganis. "You know that?"

"If my somebody can be assured by the cops and the DA that he won't get in any trouble for his adventures, I'm sure he'll be glad to come forward. Does Rick have a lawyer?"

The Chief nodded. "Dodie Donawa supposedly is getting one for him. Probably her own. What's his name? Aylward? First he gets her out of the can, and now he'll try to do the same for Dodie's daughter's ex-boyfriend. Maybe your somebody should hire him, too."

"I just had a thought," said Agganis. "Maybe you put the pistol in Black's closet to get even with him for punching you in the face. Aw, shucks. I forgot. You were in the E and E Deli when whoever it was plugged Paul Fox. Oh, well. You stick around the island. Don't take any long trips. Same goes for your somebody. We may want to talk with both of you again."

"We don't plan to go anywhere," I said.

The Chief gave me a weary look. "You really don't have to go through all this 'somebody' shit, you know. The somebody is you, and we know it. You can trust us."

I nodded. "I do trust you. Among other things, I trust you to tell the truth on the witness stand. If we ever have a trial, and some lawyer asks you about this conversation, I know you'll both testify to what I just told you. You might guess who somebody is, but it would just be a guess."

He nodded. "There is that. But this somebody of yours will testify if he gets immunity?"

"I'm sure he will. He's just a wonderful guy."

"Good old somebody. People like him make America great. Come on, Dom; let's go back inside where it's warm. Do we have an extra cell for this wonderful somebody, in case we find out who he is?"

"I'll bet we can locate one," said Agganis, and they went into the building.

I walked around to the back where the Land Cruiser was parked and got there just in time to see Dodie Donawa and Norman Aylward getting out of their cars.

"Your customer is right inside," I said to Aylward. "Glad you could make it on short notice."

"How is he?" asked Dodie. "He must be miserable. I hated being in there!"

I said, "I didn't see him, but I'm sure he's fine. They may not even put up too much of a fight to keep him in. They just got some new information."

"Like what?" asked Aylward.

"They may tell you if you ask them. Is this your car, Dodie?"

She glanced at the car. "Yes. Norman stopped at my house so I could follow him down. I want to make sure that Rick is all right. Maria may have pushed him away, but I haven't. He's no killer; he's a fine young man. He wouldn't hurt a fly!"

I touched my bruised jaw. "I'm sure you're right. I'm glad you're going to spring him from the clink. I don't think he shot Paul Fox or anybody else."

"Neither do I! Come on, Norman. Let's get him out of there!"

22

I sat in the Land Cruiser and turned on the engine in hopes that the bad heater would at least take the chill away while I ran things through my head. Some day I was going to have to try to fix that heater.

It was possible, I thought, that someone totally unknown to the police or to me had shot Paul Fox by mistake when aiming for Donald. If that was the case, an angry victim of a Saberfox real estate takeover was a good bet as the would-be assassin. Sooner or later such an amateur gunman, filled with guilt or pride, would probably tell some family member or friend, and eventually the police would get a tip and make an arrest.

But how would such a person have known that Donald would be having lunch at the deli that day? Besides, we are much more likely to be killed by people we know than by strangers.

I thought about Albert Kirkland. It was possible that his death and the shooting of Paul Fox were unrelated, but whether that was so or not, Kirkland, a onetime Olympic pentathlon hopeful, had gotten himself stabbed by someone sitting in the passenger seat. Which probably meant it was somebody he'd let into his car.

Bonzo had seen Kirkland sitting in the passenger's

seat of a Range Rover and talking with someone a day or two before Paul Fox had been shot. No one at the Fireside had ever seen Kirkland in the bar, but he was in the parking lot both that day and later when he'd been killed.

Someone had driven Kirkland there the first time, the same someone who was with him when Bonzo saw Kirkland in the Range Rover. The second time, Kirkland had been the driver and his killer had either been the passenger or had met him there.

Why the Fireside parking lot?

Because the killer wasn't sufficiently familiar with the island to know a more private place, but did know that the Fireside had few customers this time of year and that even if he and Kirkland were seen talking in the car, no thought would be given to the meeting? Ergo, he'd been to the Fireside in the past.

But he'd been wrong about being ignored. Kirkland's suit and tie had caught Bonzo's attention, and because of that, he'd remembered the meeting and the Range Rover.

I drove home and looked through the Saberfox brochure that Paul Fox had given me the day before. It was a professional document, printed on thick paper and filled with first-class graphics and photos of successful-looking Saberfox executives and employees, all in suits and ties. There was a brief biography of Donald Fox and a history of Saberfox's establishment and its successes. There were quotations from satisfied customers, charts, and photos of expensive-looking properties. Very classy.

I turned the pages until I located what I was looking for: photos of the Saberfox people I knew. All of

them were there, including the late, lamented Albert
Kirkland, who was staring intently at the camera
and trying to smile.

I turned down the corners of the appropriate
pages, an abhorrent act according to my grade
school teachers, who had grown up when books
were considered too valuable to harm, but one that
didn't bother me at all in this case, and checked the
time. Somewhere the sun was over the yardarm,
and even on Martha's Vineyard the Fireside would
be open for business. A late-morning beer would
taste good on this chilly day, and I could combine
that pleasure with business. I drove to Oak Bluffs.

Max was polishing glasses behind the bar. There
were already a couple of early drinkers in a far
booth. From the scraps of conversation I could hear,
they were discussing the unpromising prospects of
the current Red Sox season. The Sox had not won a
World Series since 1918 and seemed to the drinkers
unlikely to win one this year. The general manager
seemed to be their scapegoat. It was a view I shared.
Getting rid of Clemens was the stupidest thing the
none-too-bright Sox management had done since
the team had traded Ruth to the Yankees.

It's not easy being a Red Sox fan.

"What'll it be?" asked Max as I slid onto a stool.

I got a Sam Adams and showed him the pictures.
"Any of these guys ever come in here?"

"A lot of people come in here," said Max.

"It might have something to do with the killing in
your parking lot."

"It's not my parking lot," said Max. "I just work
here." But he was now interested. "Let's have a look."

I turned the brochure so it faced him and pointed at the photos that interested me. Finally he tapped a picture.

"I don't recognize anybody else, but this guy was in here a while back." Max read the print below the photo. "'President Donald Fox and Special Assistant Bradford Hillborough.' Hillborough. That's him. Now I got a name to go with his face." Max raised his eyes to mine and leaned forward. His voice was small. "What's he got to do with that killing?"

I made my voice small, too. "I'm not sure yet, but I think maybe you should tell the cops he was in here, if you haven't told them already."

"Yeah?" Max wasn't sure.

"It might be good to have the cops owe you one."

"Yeah!" This time Max seemed more enthusiastic. Every bar can stand a little sympathy from the cops.

"You're sure this Hillborough guy is the only one of these people who's been in here?"

"Yeah. Maybe if one of them came in without a tie, I might have missed him, but not otherwise."

I found the page with small pictures of Peter Wall and Chris Reston standing in a group of other lesser lights. "You're sure about these two?"

Max squinted. "I'm sure. Never seen them in here." He flicked his eyes toward the Red Sox critics in the booth.

We were very conspiratorial. I nodded to Max, finished my beer, left the bar, and drove to the State Police station over on Temahigan Avenue. I was in luck. Dom Agannis and Olive Otero had just gotten back from their trip to the county jail.

Olive met me with a look of pain. "You again. What do you want this time?"

"Remember that you're a servant of the people, Olive. If I ever buy myself a ring, I expect you to kneel and kiss it."

"Before that'll happen, you can kiss this," said Olive, turning around and pointing a chubby finger at her broad behind.

"All right, you two," said Dom, almost smiling. "What brings you here, J.W.? It hasn't been long since you alibied a promising murder suspect. Oh, sorry. I didn't mean you, I mean 'somebody' alibied him."

"You get a call from Max, down at the Fireside?"

"No. Why would Max call me?"

"To tell you that Brad Hillborough was in the bar at least once."

"So what? You've been in there a thousand times."

"You're a hard man to help, Dom. Brad is the only Saberfox guy who's ever been in there, according to Max."

"I'll have a talk with Max. And with Bonzo, too. He sees a good deal. You got any other tidbits to feed us?"

"If not," said Olive, "you can be on your way."

"Tit for tat," I said. "Who owned the gun you found up at Rick Black's place?"

"None of your business," said Olive.

"We don't know yet," said Dom. "We think it was purchased from one of those little gun-and-fireworks places in Georgia where nothing gets written down. It's an old Walther P-38. Not my idea of a good assassination weapon at the distance between the shooter and Paul Fox, but I guess you use what you have at hand."

If you need a weapon and the only one available

172 PHILIP R. CRAIG

is a brick, you use a brick. More people have been murdered with blunt instruments than with guns or, alas for certain writers of crime fiction, with rare poisons found only in certain parts of the upper-Amazon basin.

"Any prints on the gun?" I asked.

"Wiped clean. Maybe you—sorry—maybe your somebody did the wiping."

"No. I'll bet you five bucks that Rick Black has never been to Georgia," I said.

"I know what you're thinking," said Dom. "You're thinking that—"

"I doubt if he's thinking at all," interrupted Olive. "But if he is, it can't be more complicated than that Saberfox headquarters is in Savannah, Georgia."

I gave her an admiring glance. "Gee, Olive, I've been underestimating you all these years. I didn't think you even knew Boston was in Massachusetts."

Olive stepped toward me but was stopped by Dom's beefy arm. "If you're right about all this, J.W., it means that somebody in Saberfox tried to kill his boss."

"Or his boss's brother."

"Or his boss's brother or maybe both of them." Dom nodded at Olive. "That was an early thought of ours, so we tried to find out about who inherits if Donald Fox dies. And who inherits if Paul Fox dies, too. I think it's some elderly third cousin or some such thing."

Olive forgot about me and stepped toward her desk. "I've got it on the computer. As I recall, the cousin is a lady about a hundred years old who isn't the type to hire a killer." She sat down and started tapping keys.

"Even if it turns out that this cousin tried to kill a Fox or two, was she the one who succeeded in killing Albert Kirkland?" I asked unnecessarily. "Why would cousin so-and-so do that? Kirkland wasn't in line to inherit Saberfox."

"Maybe Kirkland knew more than he was supposed to," said Dom. "Maybe he was going to spill the beans. That's a pretty common reason for getting yourself killed."

"What beans were those?" I asked.

"I wish we could ask him," said Dom. "Do you know how to use a Ouija board?"

Alas, I did not, but I had something almost as good: the Edgartown library. I got into my truck and drove there.

23

Libraries are some of the glories of the world. They are full of information, they have comfortable places to sit and read, and they are managed by people who know what they're doing and are actually pleased to help you. Almost every town has one, and I've yet to enter one that wasn't worth a visit. Edgartown's is on North Water Street, and it's a gem.

"Well, hello, J.W.," said Nancy McWiggin, who was working at the desk as I walked in the door. "Do you need any help, or are you up to it on your own?"

"I'm after information about the modern pentathlon. It's an Olympic sport, I'm told."

"I don't want to be discouraging," said Nancy, "but aren't you a little past the time when you were Olympic material?"

"Nonsense," I said. "I'm still approaching my prime, just like you."

Nancy patted her graying hair. "Maybe you're right." She smiled. "If you need help, sing out."

"I will."

But I didn't need help because I now knew how to find books using the computers that have become standard equipment in libraries as everywhere else except in my house. As the new century was beginning, I was at least entering the one that had just ended.

You learn a lot when you do research, much of it having little to do with your interests, but some of it having a charm of its own. I learned, for instance, that the tug-of-war had been an Olympic sport in the early 1900s and that in 1912, Olympic awards had been given in architecture, literature, music, painting, sculpture, and Icelandic wrestling, the last event being won, I was not surprised to note, by an Icelander. Who else would know anything about it?

I wondered how Icelandic wrestling had become an Olympic sport. Apparently some Icelander had swung a lot of weight, perhaps in the form of putting kronur into the pockets of some members of the Olympic Committee. It is an old technique but a good one that is still used nowadays, as illustrated by the selection of Salt Lake City for the 2002 games.

More to the point, I read that both the original Greek form of the pentathlon and the modern military version of it had made an appearance in those same, 1912 games.

The original Greek form had the competitors run the two-hundred-meter length of the ancient Greek stadium, throw the discus and javelin, and perform the high jump, after which the two best competitors in the four events wrestled for the championship. This original pentathlon was abandoned after 1928, leaving only the modern or military pentathlon as an Olympic event. Why, I never learned. Too many pentathlons perhaps spoiled the Olympic broth.

In any case, the modern military pentathlon survived the 1928 purge and has been an Olympic sport ever since. In theory it requires participants to contest one another in the tasks facing a mounted courier under battle conditions. These tasks include riding a horse (drawn by lot) over a five-thousand-meter obstacle course, competing with each of your rivals in épée, pistol shooting at a silhouette target, swimming three hundred meters, and running four thousand meters over an unfamiliar cross-country course.

The competition takes three days. Each country enters three competitors and the best team score wins.

Reading this, I decided that Nancy McWiggin might be right about my Olympic days, or at least my pentathlon days, being behind me, since, among other things, I was very bad at riding a horse, only a mediocre pistol shot, a flop with épée, and pretty undependable as a runner. I could swim three hundred meters without stopping, but it seemed likely that more skill than that was needed to be an Olympic competitor.

Rats.

Maybe I'd do better in the women's pentathlon. I read about it. It became an Olympic sport in 1964 and consisted of the shot put, the two-hundred-meter dash, the high jump, the broad jump, and the eighty-meter hurdles.

None of those activities was my specialty.

Rats again.

I left my books on the table, where librarians prefer patrons to leave them, so the librarians can put them back where they belong instead of on wrong shelves where they might be lost for years, and left.

"Find what you were looking for, J.W.?" asked Nancy.

"Indeed," I said. I didn't tell her that she'd been right about my Olympic prospects.

As I drove home I thought about what I'd learned. Some of it seemed helpful.

I'd had a busy morning but had missed lunch. I corrected that with a bowl of kale soup and a couple of slices of homemade white bread slathered with butter accompanied by another bottle of Sam Adams from my private stock. As I chewed and swallowed I thought some more.

After cleaning up my lunch utensils and stacking them in the rack beside the sink, I phoned Paul Fox. Nobody home. I phoned Donald Fox's office. I got Dana Hvide, the first line of his defense against would-be intruders into his inner sanctum. I told her I wanted to talk with Paul. She told me he wasn't there. I asked where I could find him. She said he was out with Donald on business. I asked her to have him call me when he got in. She said she'd give him the message. I thought she really would, since if she didn't and Paul found out about it he might be sore and complain to Donald, etc., etc.

Since I could do nothing else until I got some more information, I investigated the pantry and fridge to see what was available for supper. There was plenty, and I opted for black bean chili and corn bread. One of the good things about chili is that you can make it ahead and heat up as much as you want to use, then freeze the rest until a later meal. I was fortunate in having children who ate big people's food without hesitation (except for eggs with soft yolks and whites, which both Joshua and Diana considered abominations, just as I myself had held them to be, long ago when I, too, had been little and unenlightened).

By the time the chili was done and I had put

together a cherry tart for dessert, much of the afternoon was gone and Paul Fox had not returned my call. Crime solving would go a lot faster if people would stop making the crime solvers wait hours or days for information. Ask any detective.

He called at six, just as my family was sitting down at the supper table. I told him I wanted to talk with him about Saberfox's proclivity to employing ex-athletes, fencers in particular, and about Albert Kirkland in particular. I also told him I was sitting down to supper and asked if we could meet later in the evening. He said we could.

"Have you ever been to the Fireside?" I asked.

"Isn't that where Al got killed?"

"He got killed in the parking lot, not in the bar. Any objections to going there?"

He hesitated, then said, "No, I guess not."

"I'll pick you up at eight and we'll have a beer while we chat."

When I sat down at the table, Zee asked, "What was that all about?"

I told her I was going to have a talk with Paul Fox about the people who worked for Saberfox.

She frowned. "This isn't going to be dangerous, is it?"

"Not a chance. We're going to have a beer and talk and then we'll both go home. I'm through with doing dangerous things."

She chewed and swallowed and had a sip of the house red, then got up and walked to the gun case. She got the key off the top and opened the case and saw that my .38 was right there where it belonged. She locked the case and came back to the table.

"All right," she said.

"Ma, what were you doing?" asked nosy Diana.

"Nothing, dear," said her mother.

"When are you going to show Joshua and me how to shoot, Ma?"

Zee was by far the best shot in the family, as attested to by the pistol-shooting trophies accumulating in the guest room closet. She hated the idea of guns but loved shooting them at targets. She was what her shooting instructor, Manny Fonseca, called a natural. Life is full of ironies.

"You're still too little," I said to Diana. "When the time comes, we'll teach you. Until then, you know the rules."

Both children nodded and spoke in unison: "Don't touch a gun. Don't get in front of one. If you see one where it doesn't belong, tell a policeman or your parents."

"For that you get an extra piece of dessert," I said.

Zee and I washed and rinsed the dishes and watched the news on our tiny black-and-white TV. Nothing in the world had changed very much. At seven-thirty I got into my down coat, kissed Zee, and went out.

"Be careful," said Zee.

I drove to Oak Bluffs and pulled up in front of the Martin's Vineyard Hotel, aka Saberfox Central. Paul must have been watching for me because he was in the car almost as soon as I stopped.

"I'm not much of a drinker," he said, "but I guess I can handle a beer in a bar."

"Maria will probably be glad to know that, and so will her mom if she ever decides to stop hating you.

Neither one of them is heavy on the sauce as far as I know."

We drove to the Fireside. Because it was a cold night and the regulars were warming their innards with Max's finest, we had to drive a ways up Circuit Avenue to find a parking place. We walked back and found an empty booth against the far wall.

Bonzo was wiping down a table across the room. He smiled and came over.

"Hi, J.W. Can I get you something?"

"A couple of Sam Adams, Bonzo." I aimed a thumb toward Paul Fox. "You know this guy? Name's Paul. Paul, this is Bonzo."

Bonzo put out a thin, pale hand, which Paul Fox accepted. "Glad to know ya, Paul."

"Same here."

Bonzo went away and Paul looked at me, then at Bonzo's retreating back, then at me again.

"Bad acid," I said.

"Too bad."

Bonzo returned with two beers and we sampled them. Delish. You can't beat a cold Sam Adams.

"What is it that you want to know?" asked Paul.

"Saberfox is known for hiring ex-fencers. You know why?"

His answer suggested that he'd asked himself the same question. "I think there are two reasons. The first is that the people Donald knows best are fencers. Fencing was his life for many years, and most of the people he met were fencers. They don't drag their knuckles on the ground, if you know what I mean. They're smart and usually well educated. They're sophisticated. They can read. They think."

"Are they all snobs?"

He looked at me, then grinned. "You mean me, I guess. Well, yes, maybe a lot of them are. The ones I knew when I was fencing were a pretty proud lot. They thought of themselves as a bit above the crowd. They were fencers, not barbarians. They were gentlemen and ladies."

"Your brother never had that kind of reputation."

"He was a champion. He didn't have time for lesser men. He was a competitor. You have to have a lot of vanity to be the best at anything."

I wasn't sure he was right about that, but let it go. "So when he established Saberfox, he hired fencers because they were smart and competitive. That makes sense. Brad Hillborough fenced, you fenced, Donald, of course, fenced. Who else fenced? How about Peter Wall and Chris Reston?"

He shook his head. "No, they're my people. I brought them into the firm. They weren't fencers, but they were athletes at college. Wrestlers. Another esoteric sport, like fencing, that most people have never heard of and no one who hasn't competed can understand. Donald took my word that they'd be good employees."

"Does he still think so? The last time I saw him, he was after their scalps."

"When he found out why they were after you, he calmed down a little. If they'd acted like fools, they'd acted that way because they were trying to help me. He gave them a tongue-lashing and then a drink from his private stock of bourbon."

"Have you heard the latest about Rick Black?"

His ears went up. "No."

I told him about the planted pistol.

"Well, well," he said. "It sounds like somebody tried to set him up as a fall guy."

I watched his face and asked, "You know anybody who owns a Walther P-38?"

His hand strayed to the bruise on his chest. "I don't know much about guns. I've seen some, but not since I got here to the island. Doesn't Mrs. Donawa have one? Was it the kind you just mentioned?"

"No. That was a twenty-two that belonged to her husband."

I wondered if his honest-looking face was a countenance I should believe. Devils often pose as angels.

"Tell me about Albert Kirkland," I said.

24

"Brad Hillborough brought Al Kirkland to the firm," said Paul. "They met when Al was trying out for the Olympic pentathlon team the year Donald won the gold and Brad was Donald's private trainer. I was still in grade school, but I heard about it later."

"I understand that Kirkland didn't make the pentathlon team."

Paul nodded.

"Al was okay as a fencer, but was uncomfortable on a horse and only average as a swimmer and runner, so he never made the team. But he impressed Brad with his hard work and later Brad talked Donald into hiring him. Al was grateful and became as loyal to Brad as Brad is to Donald."

I remembered Kirkland's thin face and metallic manner when he'd come to our house with an offer and left with a threat. There hadn't seemed to be much warmth in him.

"Was he a good employee?" I asked.

Paul thought awhile, then said, "He was smart and dependable. He did what he was hired to do and earned his salary."

"Did anyone in the company dislike him?"

"Enough to kill him, you mean?" Paul shook his head again. "Al wasn't easy to like, but as far as I know nobody hated him. They worked with him but they didn't socialize with him."

"Did he socialize with Brad Hillborough?"

Paul pursed his lips. When he answered, his voice was strangely flat. "He and Brad may have gone out together now and then, but as far as I can tell Brad is really only interested in my brother's success. He doesn't have much of a social life outside of the business. His life consists of Donald and Saberfox. I believe he'd die for either one. Not much else interests him."

"How did you get along with Kirkland?"

"It was always just business. I never saw him outside of the office."

"I've heard you're in line to take over the company someday. Would you have kept him on?"

He wasn't sure. "If that happens and if he'd been as loyal to me as he was to Brad, I probably would have. I'm Donald's only family, so I'm the logical person to take over the firm if Donald retires; but if the time comes when I do take over the company, even Donald knows that our MO is going to change. I don't like this business of challenging the titles of property belonging to ordinary people. I'd stop that. Maybe Al wouldn't have wanted to work for me."

"How about Brad Hillborough? Would you keep him on?"

This time Paul knew the answer. "Brad wouldn't ever work for me. He doesn't approve of me taking over Saberfox, so if that happens he'll leave and go where Donald goes if Donald will let him."

"Why is he opposed to you taking over the company?"

He shrugged. "He was there at the beginning and he doesn't think I have the fire to keep it going. Donald runs the company the same way he fenced, with total attention. He's almost a monomaniac. Maybe that's what it takes to be a champion or to run a business. Brad thinks I'm a wimp by comparison. Maybe he's right."

I had been thinking about some of the people who worked for Saberfox. I said, "In spite of his reputation as a heartless, cold fish, your brother seems to have a knack for instilling loyalty in some people. Brad Hillborough and Dana Hvide come to mind. You, too."

Paul looked at his beer. "Loyalty is a funny thing. It can be a curse or a blessing. Saints and devils are probably equally loyal, only to different bosses."

I emptied my glass. "Come on," I said. "I'll take you home. We're beginning to talk philosophy."

He grinned a crooked grin and finished his drink, and we left.

The next morning the phone rang while I was putting the last of the rinsed breakfast dishes in the drying rack. It was Joe Begay.

"I've got some information for you. You want it over the phone or do you fancy a ride out west to Indian country?"

It was a sunny, crisp day, with a chill blue sky arcing over the brown land. A good day for a drive. It might clear my head. I'd been thinking about the case, but not too well.

"I'll come up," I said.

The wind was from the west. It was light but the waters off toward Block Island cooled it and made

Aquinnah a few degrees colder than Edgartown, so I was glad when I got inside Joe's little house with a cup of coffee in my hand.

"You ask questions about interesting people," said Joe. "A friend ran the prints on that cup and came up with a guy who hasn't been seen in more than forty years."

"Who?"

"Fella named Juan Diego Valentine. Name ring any bells?"

"No." But I instantly knew I was wrong. "Wait." My hand flew up to my forehead.

Begay waited without expression, looking like one of his ancestors watching from a rimrock as a band of Spanish conquistadors come riding north out of Mexico.

I reached back into my memory for the name but couldn't quite find it. My hand came down. Why do we put our hands to our heads when we try to think?

"Tell me what you know," I said.

Begay nodded. "Valentine was Spanish. His father and mother were both surgeons who worked for a world health organization and there was a younger daughter. The boy came to study at Tulane. Premed. Besides being a smart kid, he was a very fine athlete who seemed a sure bet for the 1960 Spanish Olympic team. He entered the United States in January of that year for his last semester at college but never showed up for his classes and hasn't been seen since. Sound familiar?"

"No. None of it." Still, the name was niggling at me.

Begay sipped his coffee. "I shall proceed, as they say in the navy. INS has his prints, but no new prints have showed up anywhere else since he disappeared.

That's quite a while between prints. How long have you had that coffee cup, anyway?"

"Not long. What else do you have?"

"Well, since my friend couldn't find any information about Valentine that was newer than 1960, he talked to some people in Madrid to see if he could find out anything that happened before that." Begay shook his head and his mouth curled up at one corner. "You probably won't believe this, but on the morning of the day Juan Diego was scheduled to fly back to the United States for his last term at Tulane, he and another young hothead fought a duel over a girl. Yeah, just like in the movies. Swords at sunrise.

"Juan Diego, being a good hand with an épée, won without raising a sweat, but had to get out of the country in a hurry. That, of course, was pretty easy because he already had his plane ticket and the others involved—friends of both parties and the girl— were slow to tell anyone what had happened. Honor and family pride and all that sort of thing. I see a little light in your eyes, my friend. You've remembered something."

"Yes. John Skye mentioned Valentine to me. Said he was supposedly the finest fencer of his day even though he'd never won a major championship of any kind."

"And you now have his coffee cup in your possession. Congratulations."

"What happened to the loser?"

"He seemed dead for sure, but wasn't. He recovered and he married the girl. How could she say no to a man who'd been willing to die for her? So much for the benefits of being the finest swordsman in Spain. As I recall, Cyrano didn't get Roxanne, either.

You want to tell me anything about where and how you got that coffee cup?"

"I take it that when Valentine got to the United States he figured that the Spanish authorities would want him back to face homicide charges, so instead of going to Tulane, he decided to disappear."

"So it would seem. There are thousands of illegal immigrants in this country. It's just that he's been around longer than most. He is still alive, isn't he?"

"If I tell you, I'll have to kill you. Do you fence?"

"You mean with foils and sabers and like that?"

"Yes."

"No."

"We must be the only two people in the world who don't."

"I had a bayonet when I was in the army. Does that count?"

When our families had partied on the beach together I'd seen a few scars on Joe's body that hadn't been there when I'd known him in that long-ago war where we'd met, so I had reason to believe that his current, unofficial work, whatever it was, obliged him to know more about cutting-edge weapons than he might admit.

I said, "I don't think a bayonet is quite the same thing. I'm surrounded by swordsmen. It's weird. For years I only knew one, John Skye, and now I've got them coming out of my ears."

We drank our coffee.

"You need any more information about anybody?" asked Joe.

"Probably, but I don't know what it is."

As I went out to my truck, Joe said, "Remember that Confucius say guns and swords are safest when you're standing behind them and maybe a little bit to one side."

I thanked him for his wisdom and drove home, where I put a pair of latex gloves and some tape in my jacket pocket before driving to Oak Bluffs, where I found Paul Fox outside the Saberfox offices. He said he and Brad Hillborough were just going out to join Donald at the site of a prospective purchase.

"Where was Al Kirkland staying before he met his maker?" I asked.

Paul told me but added, "You can't go in the house because the police still have that yellow tape up. I guess the detectives don't want anyone disturbing evidence."

My guess was that the detectives had probably already disturbed whatever evidence might have been there. I told Paul that all I wanted to do was check out how long it took to drive from Kirkland's rooms to the Fireside parking lot. Paul wondered why that might be important. I told him I wasn't sure it was, but it might be.

In my rearview mirror I could see him watching me as I drove away.

Al Kirkland had lived in a winterized cottage off Barnes Road, not far from where John Reilley lived in his underground home. I parked nearby and put on the latex gloves while I studied the neighborhood. There weren't many people around. When there were none in sight I used my lock picks and slipped inside the house, neatly ducking under the yellow police tape. It was my third successful illegal entry in less than a week. Maybe I had a genuine talent for a career in crime. It was worth thinking about.

25

Kirkland's place had that empty smell of uninhabited rooms and revealed little of his character or personality. The house had been rented furnished, and Kirkland had made no effort to personalize it in any way. His clothes still hung in a closet, his suitcase was still against a bedroom wall, and his razor and toothbrush were still in the cabinet over the washbasin in the bathroom. A ballpoint pen and some sheets of notepaper were in the drawer of the bedside table, and a half-read paperback novel lay open and facedown on top of the table. When Kirkland had left home for the last time, he'd apparently had no reason to believe he'd not be coming back.

Not much seemed to have been disturbed by the police, although the furnace had been turned down until it was just warm enough to keep the pipes from freezing.

There were no business papers and there was no sign of his laptop computer.

I pawed through the clothes in the closet and through those in the bedroom bureau. I found nothing of interest. I peeked under the mattress and rugs and opened every cabinet I could find.

I looked through the refrigerator. Not much there. Kirkland, a lone male, apparently ate out instead of at home, as did many of his ilk. He could have saved himself some money and enjoyed some great meals if he'd learned how to cook. Too late now.

I didn't think the detectives had done much more detecting than I had. Why should they?

But just to be sure, I pulled out the drawers of the bureaus and peeked under them and behind them before replacing them, and looked behind whatever furniture was backed against a wall. Nothing.

Fine. Just because Kirkland had left no secret documents didn't mean he couldn't have left one in a place the cops hadn't found because they had no reason to look hard enough. I was sorry that his computer was gone. The cryptic message I planned to write might have seemed more authentic if it had been typed on his laptop. Ah, well, it's an imperfect world. The notepaper in the drawer of the bedside table would have to do.

Using the ballpoint pen and printing in block letters I wrote the brief document I had in mind. I addressed it to Donald Fox, dated it the day of the shooting, and printed out Kirkland's name at the bottom since I had never seen his signature. A poor fraud, but it would have to do. I folded the sheet, addressed it once more to Donald Fox, and taped it underneath a drawer of the bureau. An anonymous phone call to Fox should get the note into his hands, after which interesting things might happen.

I searched my conscience for guilt and found none. If I was wrong I could straighten things out later; if I was right, a lot of pressure would be put on a murderer.

I was going toward a window to check the emptiness of the street before leaving when the front door opened and Brad Hillborough limped in. I felt a chill that had nothing to do with March weather.

He pointed his cane at me and said, "Hello, there, Mr. Jackson. Surprised to see me?"

I was, but shouldn't have been. "I really should learn to lock doors behind me," I said. "I presume you've been talking with Paul Fox."

He looked around the room. "Yes. Little brother told me of your curiosity about Albert's house. I didn't believe the part about you only being interested in the distance from here to the Fireside parking lot. So here I am. Why are you really here?"

I'd anticipated the question. "I can't imagine why I should tell you that," I said. "Now, if you'll excuse me." I stepped toward the door.

He pushed it shut behind him and put his back against it. His face was chiseled and his eyes were bright and cold. "I think the police will be interested in why you've broken in here. If you don't explain your actions to me, you'll certainly be obliged to explain to a judge and jury."

"I'll be glad to do that," I said. "I'll tell them that I saw you break in and followed you to keep you from destroying evidence. I was just a citizen doing his best to prevent a crime."

He actually smiled. "And when I tell them the truth, who will they believe?"

"We'll find out, won't we?" I stepped closer.

He didn't move. Instead he gripped his cane with both hands. The end of its handle was a solid knob of silver large enough, I thought, to brain anyone its wielder might want to brain. I wondered if his limp would slow him down enough to lessen the advantage the weapon gave him.

I stopped. But even as he gripped the cane, he was thinking.

"Why would I want to destroy evidence?" he asked. "What evidence?"

A change in my plans instantly occurred. "I was about to find out when you came in," I said. "I've looked in the obvious places and was about to look in the less obvious ones. The ones I suspect the police never investigated."

He was thoughtful. "What do you expect to find?"

I shrugged. "Something about the shooting of Paul Fox. Maybe Kirkland kept a diary."

He eyed me carefully. "If there was a diary, the police would have taken it. Why do you think that Albert knew something about that shooting?"

"He was killed for a reason," I said. "He was seen in the parking lot behind the Fireside a couple of days before the shooting, talking with someone in one of those green Range Rovers you guys favor. The night after the shooting, he gets himself killed in the same parking lot. He never went inside the Fireside in all the time he was on the island, but twice he meets somebody in the parking lot, with Paul Fox getting himself shot in between meetings. That's a lot of coincidence, don't you think?"

He shook his head. "Not enough to bring you here."

"There's more. Kirkland was a pentathlon competitor back when you met him, according to Paul Fox and you."

"So?"

"So he wasn't good enough to make the Olympic team. He wasn't much of a rider and only a so-so runner and swimmer. Is that how you remember him?"

Hillborough turned the cane in his hands. "More or less."

"According to Paul Fox," I went on, "Kirkland was all right as a fencer, but he had to be good at one of the five sports to think he had a chance. Paul didn't mention Kirkland being bad at pistol shooting, so I'm guessing he was good at it. They shoot air pistols in Olympic competition, but a pistol is a pistol and, if I'm right about Kirkland being good with one, that makes him a real candidate as the shooter, because whoever plugged Paul Fox put two thirty-eight slugs into Paul's chest right above his heart, and from a pretty good distance. It would take a good shot to do that."

Hillborough shook his head. "The shots were meant for Donald, not his brother. It was the opposite of good shooting—it was terrible shooting."

I put casual conviction into my voice. "No, the shots were for Paul. It wasn't a mistake. Kirkland knew what he was doing, and if Paul hadn't been wearing that vest that no one knew about, he'd be dead as you can get."

Hillborough's eyes became oddly veiled. "That's nonsense. Why would Al Kirkland try to kill Paul?"

"People kill people for a lot of reasons." I pretended to survey the room. "I came here to see if Kirkland left something behind that might tell us just what you want to know. An insurance policy of some kind."

"What do you mean by an insurance policy?"

I moved away from him. "I mean something to protect himself in case he was threatened."

"I don't follow you."

"Of course you do. Kirkland was killed shortly

after the attack on Paul Fox. He may have sensed that he was in danger and decided he needed a defense. As it turned out, his insurance policy, if he had one, did him no good. But if it exists and if we can find it, it might tell us who killed him."

Hillborough's expression was wary, but he left the door and limped to the center of the next room, looking here and there as he moved. "Who did he fear? And why? Was it some angry property owner? There are such people, as I know all too well." His voice had a bitter tone.

"Yes," I said, "you know about such people. But as far as I know, Dodie Donawa is the only islander who's come after anybody working for Saberfox, and she was only after Paul for courting her daughter. No, I think somebody in the company got Kirkland to shoot Paul, then killed Kirkland to keep him from talking about it. I think Kirkland may have tried to protect himself by creating a document of some sort identifying the person who was behind the attack." As I talked, I looked under pillows and pulled furniture from the walls and pretended to pay no attention to Hillborough.

Hillborough began looking into cupboards. "You're full of conjecture, aren't you? If Kirkland had such a document, why didn't it work? Why didn't it keep Kirkland alive? You're guessing, and guessing badly."

But he kept on opening doors and peering inside them.

I stood in the middle of the bedroom and scratched my head as I looked around. "I don't know, but I can think of a couple of possibilities. Maybe the killer figured he could find the document before anybody else did, or maybe Kirkland got killed before he could say that he had one. A weapon is only a deterrent if the enemy knows you have it."

Hillborough's lip curled. "Or, more probably, there was never such a document in the first place."

I nodded agreeably. "Well, so far that seems to be the case. But we've just gotten started."

For the next fifteen minutes I looked in wrong places, just to make my search seem legit. Then, when I finally peeked beneath the correct drawer and muttered, "Eureka," I made sure that Hillborough was near enough to hear me.

I pulled the folded paper off the drawer and put a smug smile on my face. "Well, well, what have we here?"

Hillborough limped swiftly to me and reached out a hand. "Let me see that!"

"Hold your horses!" I said, but he snatched the paper from me.

"Get back!" he cried, shaking his cane in my face.

"That's addressed to your boss, not to you," I protested, stepping back. "But the police should really have it."

He stared at the paper, then suddenly unfolded it. As he read, he paled. I took two side steps toward the door.

"A forgery!" he cried. "Al Kirkland never wrote this! It's a trick!"

"What is it?" I asked, putting out a hand. "Let me see."

He hobbled backward, keeping between me and the door. "Get away! This is none of your business!" But then his eyes widened. "Wait! You wrote this, didn't you? Of course you did! You want Donald to read it so he'll turn on me. You slime! You're worse

than the others. Well, you won't get away with it."
He thrust the note into a pocket. "Donald will never
see this!"

"Why? What does it say?"

He stepped toward me. There was a cold madness
in his voice. "You know! You know!" He gripped his
cane with both hands.

There was a light wooden chair about three feet
behind me and to my left, and I thought I could get
to it before he could reach me with the silver head of
the cane.

"Let me guess," I said. "It says that you gave
Kirkland the orders and the pistol to kill Paul. It
says that you hate Paul the way you hate everyone
else who comes between you and Donald. It says
you don't want Paul to take over the company and
turn it into something different, something unlike
what Donald has made it, and that you won't let
that happen because it's not what Donald really
wants, and that you've got some sort of sickness that
makes Donald the center of your whole world. It
says that Donald is the only person, the only thing,
you love. It says that Kirkland is sorry about shooting Paul but is afraid of you, and that if anything
fatal should happen to him, the police should arrest
you for murder.

"Or words to that effect. How am I doing?"

"It's a forgery! Kirkland never wrote it—you did!"

"I don't really need the note," I said. "All I need is
a quick talk with Donald and the police. I'll tell them
what's written in that letter. They can take it from
there. Donald will know that it's true and he'll never
forgive you because he loves his brother even more
than he loves Saberfox. You and he are through."

"You're not going to tell anything to anyone," he said, and he twisted the handle of his cane. Out of the cane came a glimmering steel blade, and as it leveled toward me, he lunged.

— 26 —

A straight lunge is the fastest way to get the point of a sword into its target, if the distance is right. I'd learned that much in my brief experience as a fencer wanna-be. And the distance was right for Hillborough. But if the target is moving backward fast enough as the lunge comes, the point will arrive in empty air, and even as Hillborough's blade was hissing out of the cane, I was jumping away.

I was shocked by the blade because I'd been expecting Hillborough to strike a blow with the silver ball on the cane's handle, but my leap backward carried me to safety.

Hillborough cursed and recovered forward, impeded by his damaged leg but moving swiftly. He came slashing after me, the action showing me that his sword had a cutting edge as well as a point. I snatched the wooden chair and swung it up in front of me as a shield. Paint and wood chips flew as his blade lashed the wood.

The door to the living room was behind me and I backed through it. On my left was the door to the porch, but I didn't know whether or not Hillborough had locked it behind him. If he hadn't, I might make it outside. If he had, I'd have no time to open it before he was at me.

Hillborough lurched into the living room and lunged low, beneath my shielding chair. I avoided the thrust only by jumping back and to my right, and Hillborough scurried between me and the porch door.

But he couldn't be everywhere. Behind me now was the kitchen so little used by Albert Kirkland. On its far wall was a back door. The door was also surely locked, but the kitchen had other attractions.

For a moment both Hillborough and I paused and panted for oxygen that suddenly seemed scarce, then I retreated into the kitchen and finally had weapons of my own: knives both large and small. I plucked a large one from the magnetic holder on the wall as Hillborough came limping after me.

"Be careful, Brad," I said, holding the chair in my left hand and the knife in my right. "I may not know anything about swords, but I'm a fisherman, and fishermen know a lot about knives."

"Fuck you. A knife is just a short sword and I know more about swords than you do."

He lunged but I caught the point on the bottom of the chair. I swung the chair to one side in hopes of snapping the blade but his recovery was too fast. He shifted his feet and studied me with cold, diamond-hard eyes, the tip of his blade making tiny circles in the air.

"You may have gotten Kirkland with that pig-sticker," I said, "but I'm not Kirkland. I wasn't taken by surprise."

"Albert was easy," said Hillborough, taking breaths as deep as my own. "You'll not be much harder."

I rued the locked rear door. It's always more frustrating to be close to your heart's desire than far from it.

Hillborough thrust at my chest, but halfway through his lunge, as I swung the chair as a shield, he dropped his point to my knee. I jerked my leg back too late and felt the point strike my thigh. I swung the big knife at his arm but he was too fast with his recovery. I glanced down and saw blood on my pant leg just above my knee.

"Touché!" said Hillborough mockingly. He extended his arm and pointed his sword at my eyes. Tiny lights seemed to dance from its needlelike tip.

I threw the knife at him, but as I did he bent his arm, lifted his point, and easily parried it aside. I snatched another knife from the rack.

"Was Kirkland threatening to name you as the mastermind of that botched try at Paul Fox?" I asked, panting. "Or did he just want more money to keep his mouth shut?"

Hillborough made another feint and I moved my chair in front of his point. He nodded as if that was what he'd thought I might do. "Neither," he said. "Albert was perfectly loyal and he wasn't greedy. It's just that when the plan went wrong, he became concerned about discovery. He wanted to talk with me, to be reassured. It made it very easy to kill him. One thrust at close range."

"You're pretty cold," I said. "He trusted you."

"Ah, but I didn't trust him. He had to go, and now so do you. Donald must never know about any of this business."

He attacked ferociously, and amid flying chips of wood and paint, I was forced to leap back nearly to the door as I barely deflected the sword blows with the chair. It was getting heavier by the minute and I was getting slower swinging it. Hillborough stepped back and eyed me.

His voice was almost theatrical. "You have run out of retreating space and I am about to end the refrain and thrust home, as another swordsman once said. Good-bye, Mr. Jackson."

I threw the second knife but again he neatly parried it aside as I grabbed a third one. He smiled without warmth, extended his arm, and stepped forward. I threw the third knife, and once more, seemingly almost bored by my unimaginative attacks, he bent his sword arm, lifted his point, and made an easy parry.

But this time as he parried I thrust at his sword with the chair and leaped toward him. The chair legs tangled with his blade, carrying it aside. He tried to jump back but his bad leg failed him, and in an instant I was inside the long reach of his sword. I dropped the chair and caught his sword wrist with both hands.

We swayed and fought and he beat at me with his free hand, but I was the bigger man and at last I tore the sword from his grasp and threw it across the room.

He caught up a heavy glass ashtray and crashed it against the side of my head. The world went gray and whirled around me. I hit him with a weak fist and he came back again with the ashtray. The gray turned black. I was in a room but I couldn't see it. I got an arm up in time to catch the next blow from the ashtray. What a fate: to save myself from a sword, only to be killed with an ashtray.

But he no longer had the ashtray. Somehow it

had been separated from him. My vision came back enough for me to see him as he shoved me away and scrambled awkwardly after the sword cane.

I threw the wooden chair at him and it knocked him down, but he was up again instantly and hobbling swiftly to the far corner of the room. I got my feet moving and managed to get to the front door. It wasn't locked after all. I went out in a rush, slamming the door behind me. The cold air was a tonic. I made a shuffling run to the Land Cruiser, got in, and started the motor. Parked directly behind me was a green Range Rover.

I looked back at the house. Hillborough was lurching rapidly along the walk in front of the house, coming toward me, sword in hand.

I got the truck into gear, put the gas pedal to the floor, and left the smell of burning rubber behind me for Hillborough to inhale. In my rearview mirror I saw him heading for the Range Rover.

I drove fast to Saberfox's office, peeling off my rubber gloves en route and stuffing them into the pocket of my coat. Dana Hvide was at her desk. She was cool as ever but kept looking at my bloody face. No, she didn't know where Donald was. Paul and Brad knew and had gone to join him.

I didn't have time to be gentle. I reached over her desk and dragged her across it to my side. She opened her mouth to scream, but I covered it with one hand as I shook her with the other. I tried not to shout.

My bloody head was what convinced her I was telling the truth as I described my encounter with Hillborough. When I took away my hand she told me where to find Donald.

"Call the police and tell them what's happened," I said, "and don't let Hillborough near you. If you hear from Donald or Paul, tell them what I've just told you. I think they may both be in danger. Certainly Paul is. I'm going to try to get to them before Hillborough does."

I ran down to the Land Cruiser and broke the speed limit getting to Katama. Naturally there wasn't a cop in sight to come racing after me, siren howling and blue lights flashing. I wished I had my pistol.

Donald Fox was at a development site not far from Herring Creek. From the deck of the house he was planning to steal, you could see South Beach and the Atlantic Ocean rolling over the curve of the earth toward the far-distant Bahamas.

I got there late.

There were already three green Range Rovers pulled up side by side in the driveway, and Brad Hillborough was lurching, cane in hand, toward the Fox brothers, who were standing on the lawn looking at him curiously.

I pounded on the horn and swerved into the yard, trying to get between Hillborough and the Foxes. But at the last moment I saw the trench of a new sewer system between the lawn and me and had to slam on the brakes to keep from sliding into it.

I jumped out of the truck and shouted, "Run, Paul! He wants to kill you!"

I leaped over the trench and ran after Hillborough, shouting words I don't remember.

But Paul Fox didn't run. He stood there, stunned, as Hillborough reached him, whipped the blade from the cane, and lunged at him.

But Donald was as quick as Paul was slow. As Hillborough lunged, Donald shouted, "No!" and stepped in front of the sword, taking it full in the chest.

The blade bent and Donald Fox fell. Hillborough recovered from his lunge and stared with horror as Fox's coat began to turn red.

"Run, Paul!" I shouted, as I closed on Hillborough. "You're the one he's after!"

But Hillborough seemed to have forgotten about Paul. He stared at Donald, who lay on the lawn, and stepped away as if in a daze. I got between him and the Foxes, but he paid no attention to me.

"What have I done?" he asked abstractedly. "What have I done?"

"Put down the sword," I said, looking around for some weapon to enforce my demand but finding none.

"Christ," he said. "Wilde was right." He turned and walked off a few steps.

Then he put the silver ball of the cane on the ground and fell on his sword.

— 27 —

As I watched Hillborough fall, I heard a groan behind me and turned to see Paul Fox holding his brother in his arms while Donald touched a hand to his own chest and brought it away red with blood.

But Donald was alive.

In the distance I heard the sound of sirens. Dana Hvide had given the police both my story and directions to this location.

"Help is on its way," I said.

Paul Fox cradled his brother in his arms. "Take it easy," he said. His face was white.

"I think I'm all right," said Donald. He gripped his brother's hand. "I've been wearing Kevlar for a week now."

I opened his coat and there was the armor. Hillborough's blade had gone through it far enough to bring blood, but apparently not too far.

The brothers smiled at each other.

I rose and walked to Hillborough's body.

There's a thin line at best between the willingness to commit suicide and the willingness to commit murder, and sometimes there's no line at all. I had read about ancient warriors throwing themselves on their swords, but I had never imagined I'd see it happen.

For some reason I thought of Yukio Mishima, the

Japanese writer who disemboweled himself when a regiment of soldiers laughed at his efforts to lead them into fanatical nationalism, and I wondered if most suicides were similar failures of romance. Maybe love had killed both Hillborough and Kirkland, and had come close to killing Paul and Donald Fox. It could be a dangerous emotion.

I walked back to the Foxes and stood beside them as the police cars and ambulance arrived.

I was home when Agganis called and asked me to come and see him.

Before nurse Zee would let me do that she sat me in a chair, took off the bandage the medics had put on my head wound at Katama, cleaned the area again, and applied a new dressing. Then she did the same for the puncture wound in my thigh.

"You should go to the hospital right away," she said.

"I'll go after I see Agganis," I said, standing up.

"You need to be X-rayed," she said, "although I'm not sure they can x-ray a rock. I thought you told me you were going to stay out of trouble!"

I tried humor. "Because I did not stop for harm, it kindly stopped for me."

Zee was not amused. "You're a terrible example for our children!"

"They still like me," I said in a small voice.

"I think I'd better drive you up there. The kids can come with us."

I put my big hands on her shoulders and looked down into her worried eyes. "I'm fine. I drove here and I can drive there."

She put her arms around me. "I worry about you."

"I'm glad you do."

Agganis was in his office with Officer Olive Otero. "You want to tell me what happened between you and Hillborough?" he asked.

"Sure," I said. I then lied about who'd gone into Kirkland's house first, didn't mention having written the note, but told him most of the truth about the fight between Hillborough and me and about what had happened after I had gotten away from him.

Agganis listened and then said, "So after you got away you went to the Saberfox offices first, to warn the Fox brothers, then went down to Katama. Is that your story?"

"That's it."

"Paul Fox says you asked him how to get to Kirkland's house and that he didn't give that information to Hillborough until fifteen or twenty minutes later. Now you say you followed Hillborough into the house for fear he'd destroy evidence. Where were you for that twenty minutes?"

"Driving from the house to the Fireside parking lot. I wanted to know how long that took. After I got to the lot, I went back to Kirkland's house to do it one more time just to be sure. That's when I saw Hillborough going in and followed him."

Agganis gave me a sour look. "I can't prove it didn't happen that way. Can you prove it did?"

I feigned innocence. "What do I have to prove? Maybe somebody saw me at the Fireside parking lot."

"We'll ask. Why did you want to know how long it takes to get from Kirkland's house to the Fireside?"

"Because Kirkland met somebody in the parking lot in the other guy's car a couple of days before

Paul Fox was shot. Bonzo saw him in the passenger's seat. But he was driving his own company car later when he got himself killed. The evening Kirkland got killed there wasn't another car in the lot, which probably means that whoever he met there was either a passenger or arrived on foot. I wondered if the guy on foot had called Kirkland and told him where to meet him and if he did, how long it would take Kirkland to get there. The answer is about ten minutes. Hillborough lived in the Martin's Vineyard, which is about that far away from the parking lot, if you walk."

"That's true of a lot of the people who live in OB. Why did you think Hillborough might destroy evidence in Kirkland's house?"

"He was already on my short list. Besides, why else would he break into the house? And, remember, we did find something. We found that note."

"Says who?" snapped Olive. "You say Hillborough put it in his pocket, but he wasn't carrying any note when we searched his body."

I let my surprise show, but hid my relief. "He must have destroyed it. It was evidence against him."

"So you say. Did you read it?"

"No. Hillborough grabbed it. But whatever it said, it was enough to make him try to kill me."

Olive's face was full of skepticism. "You'd lie to God himself," she said.

"You should train Olive to be more polite," I said to Agganis. "People might begin to think that all cops are as obnoxious as she is."

"Both of you, stop it!" said Agganis. Olive gave me a final glare and turned away. I coughed to cover a laugh. Agganis shook his head. "You two."

He paused, then said, "I'm pretty sure that Hillborough stashed the gun in Rick Black's house, but I can't prove it. I don't know if we'll ever get all this officially straightened out. What we know for sure is that right here in Paradise in the last several days we've had one killing, one suicide, one attempted murder, and one stabbing that looks like an accident. I think we pretty much know who did what and why, but I doubt if the case will ever be closed."

"Is Donald Fox going to make it?"

"The medics were there quick and got him to the hospital, and as far as I know the armor stopped most of the impact of the blade. Gutsy act, like him or not."

I thought of the fear that had been in me when I'd stood in front of that blade, and had to agree.

I signed a document telling my side of the story of what had happened in Kirkland's house and what I'd done immediately afterward. God might get me for that later, but Agganis let me go. I waved at Olive as I left, but she didn't wave back.

I was longer at the ER than I'd hoped to be, but at the ER you wait around a lot unless you're bleeding on their floor, in which case they take you right away. An X ray showed that my skull was in one piece, and the puncture in my thigh was clean and not too deep, so I was rebandaged at last and sent on my way.

As I drove home I wondered if any good could come out of such madness and violence and how much I was responsible for the wounding of Donald Fox and the suicide of Brad Hillborough. I decided I could live with Hillborough's death, but I was bothered by Fox's wound. I didn't like Fox, but if I'd not had my confrontation with Hillborough, he might not have snapped and accidentally stabbed the man he loved more than he valued his own life.

Or had it really been an accident? Was it Freud who suggested that there are no accidents, but, rather, that what we do we do for reasons buried deep within us?

I thought back to my encounter with Paul Fox earlier in the day. He'd mentioned that he and Brad Hillborough were about to join Donald Fox at the site of a prospective purchase. If I'd asked him where that was, he probably would have told me, and I'd have known where to go to warn both of the Foxes that Hillborough was on the loose.

But instead I'd asked for the location of Kirkland's house, and because of that one man was dead and another stabbed in the chest. Thus large events turn on small ones. It was another case of the kingdom being lost for want of a nail.

The children were in bed by the time I got home, but Zee was up and wide-awake, full of questions.

I got us each a brandy and we sat on the living room couch in front of a dying fire in the stove I'd installed just before our wedding in an attempt to make my sometimes chilly old bachelor camp into a place suitable for a married couple to live during the winter.

I pushed my lock picks and practice locks to one side so we could put our feet on the hatch cover that served as our coffee table. I told her what I'd told Agganis and what Agganis had told me.

When I was through, she said, "So Brad Hillborough hated Paul Fox and got Kirkland to shoot him, then killed Kirkland to keep him from talking about it."

I nodded. "So it seems."

"And you figured that out."

"I thought that the shootist was probably somebody in the organization, because he knew where Paul Fox was going to be and had established an escape route for himself ahead of time. If I'd remembered that Brad Hillborough actually admitted that he'd made the plan to go to the E and E, I could have saved myself a lot of time and effort, but I didn't."

"It's a good thing that Paul was wearing that vest."

"Amen to that, because the bullets that hit him were very accurately fired. When I learned that Kirkland was brought into the company by Hillborough and that he was a good pistol shot, I thought about Hillborough's fanatical dedication to Donald Fox.

"I don't know what the shrinks would call that kind of devotion, but they probably have a name for it. Whatever it's called, as far as Hillborough was concerned anybody who got between him and Donald or between Donald and what Donald wanted was an enemy."

"And Paul fit that bill."

"Yes."

"Ten-cent psychology," said Zee. "But then you found that note in Kirkland's house."

"That's what I told Agganis," I said. "There was a note and what it said was enough to push Hillborough over the edge. Apparently Hillborough destroyed it between the time he tried to kill me and the time he stabbed Donald Fox. But there's more to the story."

"Tell me," said Zee, and I did that.

She was quiet for what seemed like a long time, then she put her arm around me. "I'm glad you had that chair."

I sipped my brandy. "It's too bad I couldn't have stopped Hillborough there in the house. He came within a whisker of killing Paul before he killed himself."

"But Donald stepped in front of the sword and saved Paul just like Hillborough shoved Donald from in front of that car years ago. Crazy." Zee laid her dark head against my shoulder.

"I believe that's a politically incorrect term these days," I said, "but it seems appropriate. Shall we go to bed?"

"Yes. We can test whether the penis is mightier than the sword."

"Is that an original pun, or did you steal it?"

"Do you care?"

"No."

"Do you want to participate in the test?"

"Yes."

"Well, come on, then!"

We went.

— 28 —

The next morning Zee phoned me from the hospital and said that Donald Fox was definitely going to live. He was a tough man in good physical condition. The sword blade had stopped short of his heart and major arteries but had punctured a lung and sliced through lesser blood vessels. They'd operated and repaired most of the damage. Paul Fox was by his side, and Maria Donawa was by Paul's side as often as she could slip away from her duties for a few minutes.

"Bad news for Dodie," I said.

"Dodie will just have to get used to it," said Zee. "Besides, Paul is not the kind of man Donald is. He's a nice guy. Maria told me that he told her that Saberfox will only take Dodie's house over his dead body. The boy has spunk he may not have known about."

"He's in love with Maria," I said, "and love is transforming. Take me, for instance. Before I knew you I was just a lazy guy who was only interested in beer and fishing. I didn't have a steady job, and I was totally without ambition. But then I fell for you, and look at me now."

There was a long silence at the other end of the line.

"Hello?" I said. "Hello? Hello? I think we've been cut off."

"I'll see you tonight," said Zee hoarsely.

The next day I drove up to John Reilley's work site and joined him on a pile of two-by-fours as he ate lunch under the noon sun. On the lee side of the house it was almost warm.

I told him about Hillborough and the Fox brothers, and about Maria and Paul.

"So Hillborough and Kirkland played Iago and Roderigo, eh?" said John, shaking his head. "Well, they're gone now and won't be missed. I wish good luck to the kids. Maria needs someone to take her mind off her mother's life, and young Paul may be just the man to do the job."

"Maybe you can do the same for Dodie. She fancies you and she's going to need somebody to keep her from fussing about Maria and Paul."

He looked sad. "I fancy her, too, and I think I could distract her or maybe even get her to change her mind about Paul, but I suspect that I should be moving on. I've been on the run for forty years, and I'm tired of it, but I have my reasons for going and they're good ones." He bit into his sandwich.

"Maybe not as good as you think," I said. "The lad you ran through didn't die. He got better and married the girl. You're not a wanted man and never have been."

He chewed but had a hard time swallowing. "What are you talking about?"

"I'm talking about Juan Diego Valentine, who fled from Spain to the United States, thinking he'd killed a man, and disappeared." I told him what I'd learned from Joe Begay.

He shook his head as though in a daze. "You're

sure about this? Carlos didn't die? I was never wanted for murder?"

"Not for murder or anything else. No one involved wanted charges brought, apparently. The story of the duel got out, but the happy ending made it into a romance. The only bad part was that your parents and sister never heard from you again."

He ran a hand hard over his head. "I didn't dare write. I thought I'd disgraced the family. I wanted them to think I was dead somewhere. I've been a complete fool."

"And you've more than paid for it by being on the run all these years. Your parents are in their eighties and your sister is a grandmother, but I'll bet they'd be delighted to hear from you."

He brightened. "You think so?" But then he shook his head. "No. I don't know if I can risk it."

"If you're afraid the immigration people will kick you back to Spain, don't be. I'm not going to tell them you've lived here illegally for most of your life, and I don't think your family will rat on you. They'll just be happy to know that their long-lost son is alive and well. Hell, you've been John Reilley for so long that you can probably go see them on an American passport."

"I don't have an American passport."

"I'll bet you can probably get one. You must have a Social Security card, since you've been working for forty years, so you must have a birth certificate, too, because you'd need that to get your SS card. That should be enough ID, unless they're both fakes. So tell me: How did you become John Reilley? It's a short step from Juan to John, but where did the Reilley come from?" I arched a brow.

He was looking less and less unhappy. "Serendipity. I knew the best way I could lose myself in this big country was to change myself into someone totally different than who I'd been. So I didn't go back to Tulane for my final term as a premed student, but headed west and became an itinerant carpenter.

"I was lucky to be from a rich family, so I had enough money to see me through until I could begin earning my own, and I'd been in New Orleans long enough to speak good, Southern-style English, so nobody figured me for a foreigner on the run. I worked little day jobs at first, so I didn't need any papers, but I knew that I couldn't keep that up.

"Then one day I was in a little town in the Midwest—I won't say where—and there was a sad story on the front page of the local paper. A young man about my age had been killed by a drunk driver right outside of his church on a Sunday morning. It was exactly the sort of story that any small-town editor would put on page one.

"I read the story and learned that the family had just moved there from another little town upstate, where they had lived all their lives before moving here. The family's name was Reilley. The boy's name was John. It seemed like a kind of miracle. Out of the boy's death came my new life."

"I can guess the rest," I said.

"Sure you can. I went to that other town and got a copy of John Reilley's birth certificate. Using it, I got a Social Security card, and Juan Diego Valentine became John Reilley."

"But still, you never stayed anywhere too long. Just in case."

"I paid my income taxes because I didn't want the IRS after me, but I never got a driver's license or bought a house because I didn't want any more of a paper trail than I had to have. A moving target is harder to hit." He looked around at the greening hills of Chilmark. To the south we could see the dark blue ocean under the pale blue sky. "One good thing that came of it is that I've seen a lot of beautiful country. None better than this island, though, even though I'm living in a cave."

"Maybe it's time you surfaced," I said. "I think Dodie would like that."

"How about Maria?"

"Maria will feel just fine after I give my report," I said. "You'll get a glowing recommendation."

"You don't really know me," he cautioned.

"I think I know you well enough. You've spent forty years in the wilderness. Hell, Jesus only spent forty days."

"That's a pretty irreligious comparison."

"Some people think I'm a pretty irreligious guy." I stood up. "Time for you to get back to work."

I went to the Land Cruiser and drove home. It was almost April. Spring wasn't quite in the air, but it wouldn't be long.

Six weeks later Zee and I and the kids were on Wasque Point waiting for the blues to come in for the first time that year. Zee and I were taking turns keeping a line in the water while the kids played tag with the waves. It was one of those lovely, warm, early May days when you didn't need your waders but were comfortable in just a shirt and shorts, and the sun was a brilliant ball floating westward across a cloudless sky.

Between casts Zee brought me up to date on all the latest news, fresh from the ER hot line.

"Dodie and John Reilley are getting even cozier, and Dodie is beginning to accept the fact that Maria and Paul Fox have the hots for each other." Zee seemed very pleased by these facts, as many women seem to be when learning of engagements, marriages, and less formal linkages between people they like.

"I hear that Paul is taking over Saberfox's office here on the island," I said.

"That's right. And he's putting a stop to this practice of threatening people with lawsuits over their land. He thinks there's plenty of business for straight-arrow realtors here."

"He'll have a lot of competition. There are fifteen thousand people on this island in the wintertime, and all but a half dozen of them are realtors."

"It's not quite that bad, Jefferson. Anyway, Donald is back in Savannah, at the main office. That wound took a lot of zip out of him, but according to Maria he's got several women down there who are anxious to take care of him while he recovers. She thinks he may change his management style after all that's happened. Brad Hillborough was quite a revelation to him, she says."

"He looked at Hillborough and saw himself?"

"Something like that." She leaned closer. "And you know something neat?"

"No."

"Maria says that John has taken Dodie to his

house and that they're talking about going to Spain together. What do you think of that?"

"More proof that romance still thrives within the hearts of the bald and silver-haired crowd. And are you telling me that Donald Fox is going to become a kinder, gentler Fox?"

"Don't be a cynic. People do change, you know. It can happen."

"It certainly happened to me. Why, before I met you I was a—"

"And you still are! You haven't changed a bit! Wait! Smell that?"

I sniffed and sure enough there was a watermelon aroma floating on the southwest wind. Bluefish!

"There's the slick!" cried Zee, pointing as she grabbed her rod from the rack on the front of the truck.

She was right again. Off to the west a round, oily slick was easing toward us on the rising tide.

I snatched my rod and trotted after her down to the surf. There she made her long, lovely cast far out into the water, just in front of the slick. I put my red-headed Roberts about three yards from where her plug had hit, and began to snake the lure back to shore.

Two fish struck us almost simultaneously, swirling white water around our plugs and bending our rods. I heard Zee laugh as she hauled back and reeled down and hauled back again, and I felt the power of my fish as I did the same.

The fish didn't want to come, but they came anyway, fighting, dancing on their tails, tugging against the hooks that held them, flashing first this way and then that through the water.

We fought them into the surf, then brought them flopping and writhing up onto the sand. We hooked our fingers in their gills and carried them up to the truck where I extracted the hooks, cut their throats, and tossed them into the shade of the truck.

The children had come running, and were very impressed.

"Those are good ones, Pa!"

"Nice ones," I agreed, feeling happy. "How does stuffed bluefish for supper tonight sound?"

"It sounds good, Pa," cried Diana, who was always on the hunt for food.

"Well, let's not just stand here," said Zee, grinning. "Let's get some more!"

So side by side she and I trotted back down to the surf and made our long casts out into the beautiful, heartless, innocent sea.

RECIPES

All Delicious

SEAFOOD CASSEROLE

(Serves 8–10)

J.W. cooks this casserole in this story.

½ green pepper, chopped
½ cup onion, chopped
½ lb. mushrooms, sliced

Sauté these ingredients in 3–4 tbsp. butter, then add:

1 can cream of mushroom soup
8 oz. sour cream
3 cups cooked rice
1 lb. precooked seafood (any combination of crabmeat,
*   shrimp, lobster, scallops, or flaked white fish)*

Mix well, season with celery salt and pepper, and place in baking dish.

Top with buttered crumbs and some bacon bits (and, if you wish, green or red pepper rings, red pepper, or pimiento).

Bake at 300° or till hot, and serve.

Kale Soup

(Serves 6–8, at least)

This is a classic New England Portuguese dish that takes many forms but is always delish! Security on a cold winter's day is having a large container of kale soup in your freezer.

> *Shinbone of beef*
> *1 lb. beef chuck for stew, cubed and braised*
> *1 package onion soup mix for each 4–5 c. liquid*
> *2 medium onions, coarsely chopped*
> *1 package frozen chopped kale (or fresh equivalent)*
> *10–12 inches of kielbasa, parboiled and sliced*
> *2 cups diced potatoes and/or macaroni*
> *1–2 tsps. chili powder*
> *2–3 tsps. pesto or basil*
> *1 lb. can of boiled kidney beans or chili beans*
> *Seasoned salt and pepper to taste*

Cover shinbone with water, bring to boil, add beef, and simmer until tender (1–2 hours). Remove meat and marrow from bone and return to pot. Add soup mix, onions, and kale. Simmer till kale is nearly tender—15–20 minutes. Add kielbasa, potatoes and/or macaroni, chili powder, and pesto. When potatoes and/or macaroni are nearly done, add kidney beans.

Any other leftovers you have may be added at this time—corn, rice, green veggies, leftover soup or chili, carrots, etc. Heat until hot, and season with seasoned salt and pepper to taste.

Tom's Sausage, Beans, and Rice

(Serves 4–6)

This recipe came from Dr. Thomas Blues, retired professor, University of Kentucky. It is a simple and excellent skillet dish. J.W. uses kielbasa when he makes it but you can use hot turkey sausage if you don't eat mammals.

2 tbsp. vegetable oil
⅔–¾ lb. smoked sausage such as kielbasa, cut in 2"
  lengths
1 large onion, finely chopped
2 cloves garlic, chopped
1 tsp. oregano leaves
½ tsp. basil
Dash of Tabasco
2 1–lb. cans of red beans
Cooked rice

Heat oil in skillet. Brown sausage and remove from pan. Sauté onion and garlic until soft. Add sausage and remaining ingredients (except rice), including bean juice, cover, and simmer over low heat for about 30 minutes. Mash a few of the beans during the last 5 minutes. Serve over rice.

ABOUT THE AUTHOR

Philip R. Craig grew up on a small cattle ranch southeast of Durango, Colorado. He earned his MFA at the University of Iowa Writers' Workshop and was for many years a professor of literature at Wheelock College in Boston. He and his wife live on Martha's Vineyard.